MURDERER'S PARADISE
THE COMPLETE ADVENTURES OF
SINGAPORE SAMMY, VOLUME 4

MURDERER'S PARADISE

THE COMPLETE ADVENTURES OF SINGAPORE SAMMY, VOLUME 4

GEORGE F. WORTS

ILLUSTRATED BY
SAMUEL CAHAN

COVER BY
JOHN A. COUGHLIN

POPULAR PUBLICATIONS · 2023

TABLE OF CONTENTS

MURDERER'S PARADISE

SINGAPORE TOWN 3
MARTHANA BONDY. 12
THE WILL. 21
THE MAN IN THE SASH 30
"ALL YOURS!". 39
MURDER 47
"I WILL NOT FAIL." 54
THE VICTORY 58
1,000 TO 1 68
INQUISITION 77
LITTLE-ARROW 86
SAMMY IS TRICKED 90
REDDY TALKS 98
TOUGH CUSTOMER 104
CHINESE FUNERAL 113
STOWAWAY 124
WOMEN STICK TOGETHER 128
THE FUNERAL 139
THE DEAD MAN 155
THE ARTISTS 165
BUT IS IT ART? 170
SAM GETS TOUGH 176
SAM PLAYS THE LOVER 183

JUNGLE DEATH 195

WHAT KIND OF MONSTER? 198

SAM IS TRAPPED 203

SAM MEETS THE MONSTER. 208

MADNESS 212

ONE MORE DIES 220

KARLOV'S OFFER 229

THE END OF KARLOV 238

JEFF'S STORY 245

JUSTICE 253

MURDERER'S PARADISE

*Two men disappear from a yacht in the South
Seas—and Singapore Sammy tackles one of the
toughest mysteries of his adventurous career*

1

SINGAPORE TOWN

IT WAS THE Fourth of July in Singapore, and Singapore
Sammy was headed for trouble.

It was dark. There was no moon. Rufe Pound, his first
mate, was at the oars of the dinghy. Singapore Sammy
sat in the stern sheets. It was a two-mile pull to the beefwood thicket near Clyde Terrace Market. Off to their right,
inshore, a green light blinked on the point of Tanjong Ru.
All about them were the lights of shipping from all the
ports of the world riding at anchor. There were trading
junks and schooners, rusty-sided tramps, sway-backed
old passenger ships relegated to their final service in the
Asiatic coastwise trade, there were shining and majestic
cruise ships and liners—queens of all the seas.

Singapore Sammy, owner and skipper of the schooner
Blue Goose, was going ashore in defiance of police orders
to the contrary. Thereby hung not one but several tales.
The red-headed skipper had a large capacity for getting
himself into trouble in Singapore. He never did it mali-
ciously. It simply happened that, time after time, when he
was in Singapore, he ran foul of the police. The last time,
some months ago, when he was firmly advised to leave
town and stay away, he was told he would be clapped into
jail the instant he set foot ashore there again.

*Sammy knew he
was caught.*

In the darkness, the *Blue Goose* had anchored in the roadstead well off shore. Rufe Pound, the mate, had wrapped the oars of the dinghy in gunnysack and greased the oarlocks. He had begged to row the skipper ashore, to see him as far as Hop Fang's joint. There was bound to be trouble, and Rufe Pound stood six foot three in his size twelve socks. He was, as Sam often told him, probably the dumbest white man east of Suez, but he was as faithful as a dog, as strong as an ox, as savage, when aroused, as a tiger shark. He had been the first mate of an ore carrier in the Great Lakes, had joined an archæological expedition to the South Seas, as shovelman, and had met Singapore

Sam Shay in the course of this enterprise. He worshiped the red-headed skipper with an undying devotion.

Rufe Pound rowed with a long and tireless stroke, dipping the blades into the black water with never a splash, lifting them out at the end of the sweep with scarcely a ripple. Almost in a line with the course of the *Blue Goose's* dinghy lay the fabulous white yacht Victory, floating toy of that most fabulous of American millionaires, Oliver Baxton. Her deck and cabin lights twinkled with the brightness of water diamonds.

Singapore Sam Shay watched her grimly. Every stroke of the dinghy's oars was carrying him closer to Singapore Town and trouble. He was going ashore because he had an appointment with a friend. Jeff Carmichael, radio operator on the yacht Victory, had wirelessed him at Penang, telling

him it was a matter of life and death. And Sam Shay would
have swum through shark-infested waters if necessary to
keep that date.

The radio message had said:

MEET ME HOP FANG'S JOINT EIGHT PM
SHARP JULY FOURTH LIVES AT STAKE REGARDS
JEFF

Jeff Carmichael wasn't an alarmist. He was a cool-
headed and hard-boiled young man, as cool-headed and
hard-boiled as Sam Shay himself. Some years previously,
on a tiger hunt in Sumatra, he had saved Sam Shay's life,
running toward, instead of from, a charging tiger, stopping
the animal with the last shot in his rifle, when Sam Shay
tripped over a root and lay stunned.

That's friendship. But that wasn't all. He had lent money
to Sam when Sam was hard-pressed. He had lied Sam's
way out of jail in Rangoon. He had proved, on these and
other occasions, that he was the kind of man who stood by
a friend, no matter what the need. Hence, the red-headed
Irish owner of the schooner *Blue Goose* was defying police
orders and keeping that mysterious date at Hop Fang's
tonight.

Now and then, as he rowed, Rufe Pound would glance
over his powerful shoulder and marvel at the white yacht
and what she represented. Men could be seen moving to
and fro on the decks. There seemed to be considerable
activity aboard the yacht Victory.

"She don't stand for more'n about one day's production
o' Baxton automobiles," Rufe marveled. "I went through

that plant oncet. We unloaded a load of ore at the Baxton smelters oncet, and I spent the day in the plant. I followed the ore through to the finished car in the test yard. What got me was the automatic machines that practic'ly stamp out a whole six-cylinder engine in one blow."

Sam Shay, gazing at the looming bulk of the finest yacht afloat, was marveling, too. He knew that Oliver Baxton had been, until his death on the island of Bali a few days ago, possibly the richest man in the world. Richer than Morgan. Richer that Ford. Richer, maybe, than any Indian rajah.

It wasn't the riches of money alone. It was the riches of industrial production and power. Oliver Baxton had been the emperor of a far-flung empire. He owned the mines from which came the iron and copper which went into Baxton sixes and Baxton eights. He owned hard-wood forests in Michigan and Central America. He owned rubber plantations in South America and Malaya. He owned railroads and steamship lines. He was truly a modern emperor.

"Money ain't everything, though," Rufe Pound said largely. "What's the good of bein' the richest bird in the world if life saws you off the kind of a deal he got?"

That was true enough. All his life, Oliver Baxton had been a bitterly unhappy man. He had embarked on a cruise of the Far East a couple of months ago, and he had died in Bali a week or so ago. Sam had heard about that in Penang. It had burst on the industrial world like a bomb-shell. Accompanied by his son, his foster son, his lawyer, his doctor and his son's fiancée, he had set out, presumably, on a pleasure jaunt—the first real vacation he had taken in his life. Diabetes had killed him in Bali.

THE VICTORY WAS close now, but Rufe kept the dinghy at a safe distance, so that he and Sam Shay would not be seen in the luminous glow of her by some prowling harbor patrol. She looked, indeed, like a liner. She was a thing of power and beauty, with her white hull, her shining bright-work.

Men went into and out of doorways. Men gathered in knots on her spacious deck. It was evident that there was trouble aboard the finest yacht afloat.

Jeff Carmichael would be ashore now, waiting at Hop Fang's. Sam was very curious to know what was going on aboard the floating palace of the Baxtons'. Who would inherit the Baxton empire—an empire valued at $800,000,000—Porter, the hated son, or Ray, the beloved foster son?

The whole world was waiting for an answer to that question. The news hadn't been given out yet.

The Baxton yacht fell astern and the lights of Singapore Town drew close. Sam Shay could see the lights of Raffles Plain and Raffles Reclamation twinkling through the trees, and the lights of rickshaws dancing along Beach Road. To the right of the Reclamation was a patch of inky darkness, and this was the dinghy's destination—an uncultivated area of scraggly trees and underbrush. Here they would leave the dinghy, hidden in bushes, and from here they would go, via unfrequented streets and dark alleys, to Hop Fang's.

They had beached the dinghy and pulled it into the bushes when, close at hand, occurred the muffled hum of a motor boat's engine. The boat was running without lights, which was mystifying enough, and it was coming precisely from the direction of the Victory.

Sam caught the glint of distant lights on a hand-rubbed mahogany hull. The engine stopped and the launch came gliding in, perhaps twenty feet from the spot where Sam Shay and Rufe Pound had hauled up the dinghy.

The two men waited in the darkness of the beefwood jungle. The nose of the launch grated on the beach. Two men got out and a light flashed on. One of the men was tall and the other was short. That was all Sam saw in a glimpse.

In the winking beam of the pocket light, held by still another man, a stretcher with a man on it came into view. He was covered with a sheet from chin to toes. Gauze bandage was wrapped about his face, so that his hair and only a little of his face could be seen. His hair was yellow.

But this glimpse of a sick or dying man on a stretcher was not what caused Sam Shay to push out a little of his breath in a hardly audible grunt. The man's face was covered with reddish-black spots, like spots of dried blood. It wasn't blood. It was smallpox!

One of the men on the beach said, in a high, wheezing voice: "All right, men; get back to the ship. Tell Captain Jayne to fumigate that room immediately."

An awed voice replied: "Aye, aye, sir." The motor started, the launch backed out and became a dying vibration on the night breeze.

When the launch was well out, the high-pitched, wheezing voice said: "All right. Get up."

The taller of the two men turned the beam of a flashlight on the man on the stretcher. He threw the sheet off, yanked off the bandage, and got up with energy. He was grinning.

"Wash it off," the tall man said.

The blond man went to the edge of the beach and began scooping up water and scrubbing his face with the palms of his hands. It was a mystifying ritual. Sam Shay felt Rufe Pound's breath on the back of his neck. The mate of the *Blue Goose* was panting heavily. He was like an animal watching, in fascination, something it does not understand.

Singapore Sam was baffled only by the implications of what he saw. The flickering flashlight beam gave him occasional clear glimpses of the faces of the three men. The short man was a hunchback. He was gray-haired and he had sparkling brown eyes. He was the one who talked in a high, wheezing voice. His small, hooked nose gave him a foreign look. But the pocket light showed something else. It was importance, or power, or call it what you will. It was the quality that sets one man apart from others. It was the aura of greatness. This hunchback was, even at a glance, the most important man of the three.

His companion, the tall man, was much younger, and he was marked with another kind of distinction. It was that of masculine beauty. He was dark and handsome. With the handsomeness of his face and the leanness of his body, he was the kind who would appeal to women. He was dark-haired and dark-eyed, and he wore a crisp black mustache. He looked a little like one of our popular motion picture actors. He was that type.

The third man—he who had arisen from the stretcher—was still scrubbing his face with his palms and sea water. He turned suddenly, grinning through the wet. His small-pox spots were gone!

"Okay?" he said.

"Okay," answered the tall, handsome one.

The blond man had neither the distinction of importance nor that of handsomeness. He was an ordinary looking fellow of about twenty-eight, dressed in a khaki flannel shirt and cheap blue serge pants. He looked like a sailor. Nothing set him apart except the color of his hair—its striking yellowness.

The hunchback took his hand out of his pocket with a roll of bills. He gave it to the yellow-haired man.

"Five hundred dollars," he said.

The yellow-haired man counted the money and said, "Okay. Five hundred."

"Easy money," said the tall, handsome one.

"You understand," said the hunchback, "that you're to leave Singapore at once—and keep your mouth shut?"

"Sure."

"You're not to stay long enough to buy yourself even one drink."

"That's okay with me, gents. Can I ask one question?"

"No," the hunchback said.

"Beat it," said the tall man. "We'll wait till you're gone."

"Okay, gents. So long!"

The yellow-haired man went toward Beach Road. After an interval, the hunchback and the tall, handsome man followed.

And that was Singapore Sam's introduction to the mystery of the yacht Victory—a mystery that would transport him to the loneliest spot in the Eastern world and into the heart of a murderer's paradise!

2

MARTHANA BONDY

ON THE SINGAPORE water front, not far from Telok-Blangah Road, stands a large and rambling structure, half on land, half on weary-looking, barnacled piles over the water, across the landward face of which, in Chinese hieroglyphs, is the legend:

HOP FANG'S PALATIAL CASTLE OF HEAVENLY
JOYS AND MANY JOLLIFICATIONS

To sailing men who have patronized the place over the past quarter of a century it is known simply as Hop Fang's joint.

Hop Fang's was in its usual nightly uproar. A delegation of sailors from a French man-of-war and a delegation of sailors from an Italian submarine were holding a convention in two languages, with the same harmony that exists between a band of alley cats and a pack of street dogs.

Sailors from ships flying all the known flags were packed several deep at the bar. Women of sundry nationalities but of a single profession clung to men who hadn't seen women in weeks or months. The fantan room was packed. A six-handed poker game was going on in the card room.

Tobacco and opium smoke mingled in thick layers. The air smelled richly of sweating, unwashed humanity, of the harbor mud at low tide, of stale beer and spilled whisky, gin and *arrack*, and it smelled, above all, of Singapore.

Sam Shay and Rufe Pound reached Hop Fang's Palatial Castle of Heavenly Joys and Many Jollifications by an alley that never saw sunlight. At a black door, Sam stopped and said, "Okay, Rufe. Go out and have yourself some fun. Don't get too plastered. Be aboard by sun-up. Take the dinghy. I'll go but by sampan. We may pull out in a hurry."

"Watch out for the cops," Rufe cautioned.

"I'll watch out," Sam promised, and opened the door. He entered Hop Fang's with his heart beating rapidly and his green eyes sparkling and his grin wide with anticipation. He hadn't seen Jeff in almost a year, and it was going to be a pleasure to repay Jeff for a few of the favors Jeff had done him.

He went from one noisy, smoke-filled room to another. Jeff was not in the bar. He was in none of the gambling rooms.

He found Hop Fang in the fantan room, a fat Buddha in black satin robes, smiling like an Oriental satyr, and smoking a long black cigarette. He spoke excellent English, and he always smiled, even, Sam understood, when he was ordering a man's throat to be slit.

"Good evening, Captain Shay. If you are looking for some one, go to room fifteen."

Sam thanked him and went up the stairs to the second floor, where the private dining rooms were. These were small, dusky cubicles each containing a bare table, two chairs and a couch.

He ran down the hall to room fifteen, smashed open the door with his fist and stopped suddenly, with the grin vanishing from his lips.

A girl sat on the couch staring up at him with large and frightened blue eyes. She was not an ordinary girl—not one of the dozens downstairs. There was a certain indefinite air of breeding about her. She was no older than nineteen or twenty. She was ghostly pale. She looked like a terrified schoolgirl, with her trembling pink mouth and her clutched hands. But there was an automatic pistol in her hands.

The red-headed man said hastily: "Excuse me! I've made a mistake! I thought—"

"Wait!" the girl said huskily as he started to back out. He stopped and waited. She stood up, placed the pistol on the table and caught the edge of it to steady herself. Her resemblance to a frightened schoolgirl continued. She was trying to speak, but she couldn't. Her lips worked. She swallowed convulsively. She was a small, slim girl with her golden hair cut short and arranged in little waves all about her head. But she wasn't a schoolgirl, and her air of innocent helplessness was denied by a firm and determined chin. When her color returned, he suspected that she would be beautiful.

SHE FINALLY GOT out, in a husky whisper: "Are you Sam Shay of the *Blue Goose?* Are you the man they call Singapore Sammy?"

Sam hesitated and said, with surprise, "Yes."

"You had a date with Jeff Carmichael?" Her voice sounded surer. Her mouth was no longer trembling.

"That's right."

The girl bit her lower lip. Her eyes were swimming. She was evidently fighting off another wave of faintness.

"He's dead," she said in a weary, small voice. "He was lost overboard in the Straits of Karimata five days ago."

Without taking his eyes from that pale, lovely young face, the red-headed man shut the door and advanced to the table. Her eyes were wet and the lashes were wet, but her mouth wasn't trembling any more. Tears ran out of her eyes, but she paid no attention to them, and they ran down her white cheeks.

"You'd better sit down," Sam said gently. "Tell me about it."

She didn't sit down. "Jeff was lost overboard on the night of April sixth. It happened during a squall."

"How did it happen?"

"No one knows. It simply happened. No one saw him go overboard.—But Jeff didn't jump."

"No," Sam agreed. "Jeff didn't jump. Sit down," he repeated.

She obeyed. She let herself down to the couch, leaving the little automatic pistol on the table. Sam pulled out one of the chairs and sat down facing her. He was pale. His freckles stood out. His eyes had lost some of their greenness and were almost gray, as they became when the red-headed man was deeply moved.

The girl said faintly: "I'm Marthana Bondy. Jeff—Jeff and I were great friends. I'm Porter Baxton's fiancée."

She cried suddenly: "There are so many things I have to tell you! It's such a horrible mess!"

"Take your time," Singapore Sam said gently.

"There's so little time! I—I have to meet a man in less

than an hour—" Her voice broke again. She began beating her palms together as if to relieve her nervous distress. "Jeff told me—" She stopped and gasped for breath. "He told me if anything happened to him to keep this appointment with you. He said you'd help. He said you could be counted on. He said you were the only man in this part of the world who could really help. Will you?"

"Sure. Sure, I'll help. Don't let that worry you. Let's have the story."

Marthana Bondy's hands fluttered and fell into her lap. She sighed as if with despair. Sam Shay grimly waited.

"There's so much to tell! It's so confused in my mind! It's so mystifying! It wasn't only that Jeff disappeared. He was murdered! I know he was murdered! I saw drops of blood on the deck outside the radio room, and I saw blood on the rail where he was dragged and thrown overboard! But that wasn't all. Ray Baxton disappeared the same night at about the same time!"

Miss Bondy stopped and began trembling again. "But it doesn't mean anything, Mr. Shay, unless I tell you everything. And it's all so mixed up!"

The red-headed man realized that this girl was almost at the point of hysterical collapse. He said: "Take it easy, Miss Bondy. I'm going to help in any way I can. If Jeff Carmichael was murdered," he said with almost savage grimness, "I'll find out who it was if it takes twenty years! Did you go aboard the Victory at Frisco?"

"Yes!"

"All of you?"

"Yes. We came overland from New York by air and went aboard the Victory in Oakland. Will you watch the time?

I have to see this man and give him the money at exactly nine."

"Where?"

"In Raffles' bar."

"I'll watch the time."

"Are you sure we're safe here? I have fifty thousand dollars in American bills in this purse." She whispered the last.

He said reassuringly, "Don't worry, Miss Bondy. It's quite all right. I'm known here." He didn't feel it necessary to mention that on one of his last visits he had practically wrecked Hop Fang's Palatial Castle of Heavenly Joys and Many Jollifications, and that Hop Fang had therefore acquired a profound respect for him.

"Begin where things began," he prompted her.

SHE SEEMED TO be reassured. Her eyes were brighter and steadier, and her color was better.

"Things began to happen the first day out," she began the story of that amazing cruise. "Mr. Baxton had never had a real vacation in his life, and he took this one, so he said, to become acquainted with me, because I was going to marry his son Porter, and partly to become acquainted with Porter. That wasn't the truth at all. From the very beginning he was insulting to me. He did that and he did everything else he could to show Porter how much he hated him.

"You know, of course, that Porter is his real son, and Ray Baxton is his adopted son. They are about the same age. He always hated Porter because Porter's mother was frivolous and a cheat. She died soon after Porter was born. There was never any question that he was Porter's father. That wasn't it. They look too much alike for him to doubt it. He simply took out his hatred for Porter's mother on Porter."

"How did Porter take it?" Sam interrupted.

"It hurt him terribly. It always had. Oliver Baxton was a great man—an industrial genius and an industrial giant. Porter worshiped him. All his life, Porter has wanted to make friends with his father, but the old man wouldn't have it. And he gave all of his affection to Ray, the foster son. In his will, he left every dollar he possessed, everything he owned, to Ray; and only one dollar to Porter, just so he couldn't contest the will!"

"You have half an hour," Sam said.

Marthana Bondy bit her lower lip nervously. She cried: "Oh, there's so much I have to tell you! I can't leave any of it out. It's all important. It all has a bearing on Jeff's murder and Ray's disappearance. I've got to tell you something about the will, and something about these people. There were so many currents and cross-currents, and it's all so important."

Sam said: "Is one of these people a gray-haired hunchback?"

"Yes! He's Ben Rosen, the Baxton lawyer. He was on the trip to help the old man frame a new will. They had some awful fights about it, because Mr. Rosen sided with Porter and he had no use for Ray."

"Who's the tall, handsome one?" Sam asked.

"That's Dr. Hobb—Dr. Elton Hobb—Mr. Baxton's personal physician. He's always traveled with him. Where did you meet them?" The blond girl seemed puzzled and surprised.

"I happened to see them on the beach, bringing that phony smallpox case ashore."

Miss Bondy said excitedly: "Oh, it's all such a mess. I'll explain that in a moment. Where was I?"

"The will—the unpleasantness."

"Unpleasantness!" the girl echoed. "There wasn't a peaceful moment on the entire trip. Almost two months of insults and rows and dirty digs! Ben Rosen hated Ray, and Ray hated Porter and me, and Mr. Baxton insulted me every chance he got, and Dr. Hobb and Ray didn't get along, either. And Ray got drunk almost every night—nasty drunk. He tried to break into my stateroom, and Porter threatened to smash his head in. It went on day after day. One row after another. But when the old man died and Mr. Rosen read the will—everything went to Ray.

"It's outrageous. I'm engaged to Porter, and that makes me prejudiced, but Mr. Rosen, who is utterly hard-boiled, says what I say: Porter is the brains of the Baxton business. The old man never promoted him as he deserved. He sent Porter back to Detroit when we reached Tahiti. I stayed on, hoping I could persuade the old man to be fair. That was a mistake. Now, I'm in this horrible mess with Ben Rosen and Dr. Hobb."

She stopped again and sighed with exhaustion. "Oh, I'm so sick of it. I'm so sick of industrial empires and billionaires! Do you realize that if what I'm telling you leaked out—that Ray Baxton is missing, and that we haven't the faintest idea where he is—the New York stock market would practically go to pieces, and that the United States might tumble right into another dreadful depression? That's the responsibility on us, and that's the responsibil-

ity I'm begging you to share. If the news leaked out that
the new owner of the Baxton empire is missing and may
never be found—"

"I don't get that," Sam interrupted.

"Under the terms of the will," the girl explained, "the
Baxton estate goes to Porter in case of one of two things—
Ray's death or his turning insane. If he is dead, it must
be proved in court. You can't prove death in court unless
you can positively establish that death has occurred—the
corpus delicti. If Ray is dead, and we can't prove it, the
case will be in the courts for years. The Baxton empire will
be tied in knots. It will probably collapse, dragging down
dozens of other businesses with it. In that way, it would be
a death blow at recovery. Oh, I'm so tired of empires and—"

"What you mean," Sam said quietly, "is that you'd do
anything to find out who killed Jeff—and the Baxton
empire is a side issue."

She looked at him and her face became pink. "Yes. Jeff
was—" She stopped and breathed deeply. "How much time
is left, Mr. Shay?"

"Twenty minutes."

3

THE WILL

THE SMALL BLOND girl said breathlessly: "I think I've given you a fair explanation of what's under all the excitement. Now, I'll get on to the excitement itself. On April first, Oliver Baxton died in Bali—of diabetes. Almost his last words were that he was to be buried there. Our relief when he died was so great, and our disappointment over the will was so bitter, that—well, the strain snapped and that did strange things. Ray Baxton got drunk and stayed drunk. Ben Rosen and Dr. Hobb got drunk several nights in a row. And on the night of April 6th it happened!

"I haven't mentioned the friendship that had sprung up between Jeff Carmichael and me. He was one of the finest men I ever knew. And he used to tell me by the hour the most fascinating stories of the adventures you and he had together. If it hadn't been for Porter, I think I'd have fallen in love with Jeff."

She looked at Sam a little wistfully. "Jeff stood for the things I liked; but I've always been in love with Porter, and I've dedicated my life to Porter."

Sam suspected that she was not telling the whole truth. He suspected that she really had fallen in love with Jeff Carmichael and was miserable chiefly because of his death but bravely determined to "dedicate herself," as she put it, to Porter, for whom she had, deservedly, the greatest sympathy.

"On the afternoon of April sixth we were in the Straits of Karimata, when the lookout spied several marlin. Ray Baxton ordered the yacht stopped and one of the motor launches put overboard, which was done. He was quite drunk. So was Dr. Hobb. Captain Jayne asked me to go along, in case there was trouble, so I went. There was no trouble. They didn't catch any marlin, and we came back to the ship at sundown, and Ray told Captain Jayne not to hoist the launch back aboard, but to leave it out on a towline, as he might want to go fishing again in the moonlight.

"There was a full moon. Captain Jayne objected to leaving the launch on the towline, as the barometer was dropping and he thought there might be a squall. But Ray insisted.

"Immediately after supper, Jeff hunted me up on deck and said that some mysterious trouble was brewing. He didn't say what he meant, because Ray Baxton came along as we were talking, so that he only had time then to say he was so upset about it that he was wirelessing you to meet him here. He said that in case anything happened to him, I should meet you.

"I was not only mystified but horrified. I don't know what he knew or what he suspected, but he had been in dangerous situations so many times that I think he sensed how serious the trouble was.

"Ray Baxton was drunk, and so were Ben Rosen and Dr. Hobb. They insisted that I drink with them. I wouldn't drink, but I stayed with them on the after deck until I could get away. It was then about half past ten. I went directly to the radio room. It was empty. I was worried. I hunted all over the ship for Jeff. I looked in his stateroom, which was between decks, not connected with the radio room. The assistant radio man hadn't seen him. He had been asleep and was just getting ready for duty. I went to the galley. Jeff and I often dropped in there and raided the icebox about ten o'clock, but he wasn't there. I went back to the radio room and found the spots of blood on the deck outside the door, and followed them to the rail."

Marthana Bondy stopped again, and looked at Sam with large, forlorn eyes. She went on in a voice of disgust. "I fainted. I must have pitched forward and hit my head on the rail. When I came to, I was in my room. The assistant operator had carried me to my room and called Captain Jayne. He had tried to get Dr. Hobb, but the doctor and Ray Baxton were having a wild, drunken argument about marlin fishing.

"I told Captain Jayne about the blood spots. It must have been almost one o'clock then, and the squall was beginning. It was raining, and when he looked he couldn't find any blood spots. I don't know whether he believed me or not, but he didn't stop the ship. He said it was useless.

"I had such a splitting headache, and I felt so sick about it all, that I couldn't leave my cabin. If I'd only gone back to the after deck! If I only had! The next morning Dr. Hobb and Ben Rosen tried to tell me what had happened, or what they thought had happened, but it made a crazy, confused story. Dr. Hobb and Ray Baxton continued that argument about marlin fishing. Ray bet the doctor five thousand dollars he could go out alone in the moonlight and bring back a marlin in an hour. Then Dr. Hobb passed out. He passed out and slept all through the squall. Ben Rosen didn't pass out, but he became paralyzed. He does that when he gets just so drunk. He can see and hear and understand what's going on, but he can't move.

"There he sat, and listened to Ray rave about that silly bet. And finally Ray got out and went and got marlin tackle and pulled the launch close enough to jump overboard."

"Wait a minute," Sam interrupted. "The Victory makes about twenty-five knots, doesn't she?"

"Yes. I know what you're going to say. Ray couldn't have pulled the launch in against the drag of the water. Ben Rosen says he did it. Ray was as strong as an ox. I believe he could have done it. Ben Rosen swears he saw him do it. Then, when he was aboard, the slack in the tow-rope was taken up so suddenly that it snapped!"

MARTHANA BONDY STOPPED and stared at Sam with dilating blue eyes. Her face was flushed now; she was out of breath.

"And Ben Rosen couldn't move," Sam guessed.

"He sat there," Miss Bondy affirmed, "listening to the squall, and knowing what might happen to Ray in that small boat! Then he became unconscious. Both he and Dr. Hobb slept all through the squall, and they didn't come to until the sunrise was in their faces. Then they saw the launch and Ray were gone. And they frantically searched the ship, and they told the captain what had happened, and swore him to secrecy. Drunk as he still was, Ben Rosen realized what would happen if the news leaked out that the new emperor of the Baxton empire had been lost at sea!"

"Wasn't there a watchman on that ship?" Sam asked sharply.

"He was forward all night because of the squall and because we were going through dangerous shoals and passages between the islands."

"It sounds phony to me," Singapore Sam said.

"You haven't heard the worst of it," Marthana Bondy answered "About two in the morning, during the squall, the port engine went out of commission. Someone had tightened down on the port thrust bearing, the bearing burned out, and the speed of the Victory was automatically cut in half!"

"Who did that?"

"An oiler. I'll get to him in a moment. When Captain Jayne learned that Ray Baxton was missing, he didn't tell a soul, but he put the ship about and explained to the crew he was going back to try to find the launch. But the reduced speed handicapped us, and it was hopeless, from the beginning, to search for that small launch in that immensity of water and among those reefs and thousands of islands. We were sure Ray was dead, and that the launch had been wrecked, and that we would never find his body. That was the worst of it. None of us would have minded finding him dead—that may sound callous, but it's true."

Sam nodded. "I understand. But if you want my honest opinion, Miss Bondy, it still sounds fishy."

"It does," she agreed. "And it will sound still fishier before I'm through. Ben Rosen and Dr. Hobb were frantic. So was I. So was Captain Jayne. They were frantic because Ray Baxton had vanished, and I was devastated because

Jeff had vanished—murdered and thrown overboard—the one man— But I'll skip that.

"The three men—Captain Jayne, Mr. Rosen and Dr. Hobb—agreed that the crew must be hoodwinked. They let it be known that Ray Baxton was in his cabin—"

"With smallpox," Sam guessed.

"Yes!"

"Ray Baxton is—or was—a man with yellow hair—a big, powerful man," Sam guessed.

"Yes," she said again. "Very yellow hair. But there's something else to tell you. We gave up the search for the launch and started for Singapore. Just as we were entering the roadstead this afternoon, the starboard engine went out of commission. The same oiler who had crippled the port engine deliberately ran the starboard engine without lubrication—and it burned out its main bearings! It had hardly happened when this oiler—his name is Bruno Reddy—was off the yacht and aboard one of the sampans that came out, as they always do, to meet us. He wasn't suspected until then. But there was nothing we could do about it."

"First," Sam said thoughtfully, "this Bruno Reddy cripples one engine, then he cripples the engine room. I wonder why?"

The blond girl nodded her lovely head vigorously. "Utterly bewildering! Yes, that's why I've come to you. How much time is left?"

"Ten minutes."

"How long will it take to get to Raffles?"

"Five; finish the story."

"When we were finally towed to our present anchorage late this afternoon, Captain Jayne reported that the crew were talking. They were very suspicious. The rumor had gotten around that not only did Ray Baxton not have smallpox, but that he wasn't aboard. And once that rumor got out, there was nothing we could do. Ben Rosen hit upon that wild idea of hiring a man to impersonate Ray Baxton, smuggling him into Ray's room, decorating his face with realistic smallpox spots, then bringing him ashore, with his face covered so that little of anything but his yellow hair showed. Ben Rosen and Dr. Hobb were to come ashore immediately after I did, find such a man, smuggle him aboard in a trunk, and bring him ashore on a stretcher. What did you see?"

SAM TOLD HER what he had seen. Miss Bondy gave another of those vigorous little nods and said:

"That means, they put it over. The crew is now—presumably—convinced that Ray Baxton was in his room all that time with smallpox, and was sneaked ashore in the dead of night."

Sam was shaking his head. "It's phony and it's risky. There's a dozen rats hidden here somewhere, Miss Bondy. Somebody's lying. Maybe more than one. What do you think?"

"I'm too bewildered and upset to think. I know it's a hopeless mess. I don't know whether Ben Rosen is lying or telling the truth."

"Ben Rosen," Sam said quietly, "didn't want Ray Baxton to inherit the Baxton empire. If Ray dies and Ben Rosen can prove he is dead, the estate goes to the man that Ben Rosen wants to have it."

Miss Bondy nodded. "I've thought of that. Ben Rosen is probably the cleverest corporation lawyer in the States.

His mind is like a steel machine. That's why the Baxton corporation pays him a million a year. But if he had wanted simply to kill Ray, why didn't he do it in some clever way, so that he would have what he most wants—Ray Baxton's corpse? And why was Jeff killed and thrown overboard? Why did Bruno Reddy cripple the port engine that night, and cripple the other engine today? I don't think Ben Rosen killed Ray. He's in a terribly upset state of mind over all this clumsy duplicity we've had to resort to. This smallpox business."

"Clumsy is the word," Singapore Sam agreed.

"Ben Rosen's one fixed thought," the girl explained, "is to keep Ray's disappearance a secret. It was hard to keep it from the crew, and it will be much harder keeping the secret from the authorities and the newspaper men here. Ray Baxton is probably the richest man in the world. Where is he?"

"Does Rosen know you've come to me?"

"Yes. He authorized me to offer you any price you named to help us. He's frantic. Now I must tell you the final blow—the development that simply upsets everything. This afternoon when I came ashore, a strangely dressed man spoke to me. He wore a very full white satin shirt, or blouse, a dark-red sash and very full blue corduroy trousers. He was dressed the way eccentric artists used to dress, I believe, in Paris. His hair was long and shaggy. He was very sunburned. That's the man we're seeing at Raffles. I want you to know just how he looks.

"He whispered to me that he had some valuable information concerning Ray Baxton's whereabouts. I almost fainted with the shock. It was utterly paralyzing. Here we were, thinking that not a soul in the world but Ben Rosen, Dr. Hobb, Captain Jayne and myself knew the truth, and this perfect stranger walked up to me the instant I put foot ashore and said that!"

Sam Shay said grimly: "Just what did he say to you?"

"He said: 'I can tell you where to find Ray Baxton, if it's worth fifty thousand dollars to you in American money. Meet me in Raffles' bar at nine sharp tonight with the money—if you want to do business.'"

"Did you tell this to Ben Rosen?"

"Yes. Just before we separated. He gave me a note to the Baxton representative here, and I went to him and got the money."

Sam quickly got up. "Is that everything that fellow said?"

"Yes, Mr. Shay."

"All right," Sam said, "let's get going. I want to see this guy. He's going to do some fast explaining."

"Will you want this automatic?"

"I might." Sam pocketed it.

They went out and down the stairs and through the strong smells and uproar of the lower floor. On Telok Blangah Road, Sam secured a gharry, a horse-drawn closed cab. He preferred not to be seen by the vigilant Singapore police. He did not know how he could be useful to Marthana Bondy. But he was dead sure that whatever he might attempt to do, here in Singapore, would be made doubly difficult by his unpopularity with the police and the American consular office.

4

THE MAN IN THE SASH

AS THEY GOT under way, the girl beside him in the darkness of the jolting gharry said: "Of course, we've been theorizing ever since it happened. Why was Jeff killed? Why did Bruno Reddy cripple the engines? How does this man in the red sash happen to know that Ray Baxton vanished from the yacht? Ben Rosen is convinced that it's an elaborate kidnap plot. And this seems to prove it. And if it is a kidnap plot, it will probably be the most successful—pay the largest ransom—of any kidnaping in history. The Baxton Corporation would be willing to pay millions for him, dead *or* alive."

"Preferably dead," Sam murmured.

"Well, what's your opinion, Mr. Shay?"

He answered promptly: "How about this Captain Jayne? How about the assistant wireless man?"

"You will have full authority to go aboard and check up on both of them. If the wireless man is in the plot, he could so easily have wirelessed to this man in the red sash."

"I'll talk to them," Sam said grimly. "But first off, I want to talk to this guy in the red sash. There's a lot of questions I want to ask that guy. Here we are, Miss Bondy. You go in alone, and I will wait for you in the park—that is, in the

Reclamation. There's a path from the hotel to the water front. You bring that guy along that path. Tell him you're afraid of being seen and would rather talk to him outside. A little rough work won't make you sick, will it?"

"No," she said. "But he's a much bigger man than you are. He's big and he's powerful. And he'll probably be suspicious. And armed!"

The gharry had stopped before a large white structure which seemed to cover acres. Lights blazed in countless windows. The muted strains of a good orchestra playing a foxtrot could be heard above the soft roar of voices.

"Straight in that door and to the left," Sam said. "I'll be waiting in the Reclamation."

Marthana Bondy reached for his hand and squeezed it. "If you only knew," she whispered, "how glad I am you're in this. Good luck!"

She vanished into the hotel, and Sam instructed the *syce* to drive back along Beach Road. Half a block away he got out, paid off the *syce* and strolled to the path he had described to Miss Bondy. There was not much light here. And the thickness with which bushes grew afforded him an excellent chance to carry out his plan.

It was a very simple plan. He intended to give the mystery man in the red sash a surprise attack. He would knock him out cold. Then he would take him along the sea wall to where the dinghy was hidden in the bushes, less than a tenth of a mile away. He would take the fellow aboard the *Blue Goose* and work on him at his leisure, securing, by fair means or foul, all possible information bearing upon the murder of Jeff Carmichael and the disappearance of Ray Baxton.

The red-headed man waited beside a bush. He went over in his mind the story Marthana Bondy had told him. He was reasonably sure she had been telling the truth. Perhaps she had slighted important points, or omitted them entirely, but he would have bet his last breath on her fundamental honesty. But she was the only one of them that he felt like trusting. Ben Rosen, Dr. Hobb and Captain Jayne were unknown factors.

He watched the brightly lighted hotel and listened to the lilting music. His eyes grew used to the darkness, and when Miss Bondy appeared, picking her way uncertainly along the path, he recognized her at once. She was walking rapidly and behind her loomed a man who was quite as formidable as she had represented.

He was four or five inches taller than Sam Shay, and he was built powerfully, with a large head and tremendous shoulders.

He was saying, in a voice of suspicion: "I don't see the need of this. If it's a trick, Miss Bondy, I assure you—"

THE MAN IN the red sash was just abreast of the bush behind which Sam crouched. The red-headed man leaped out. He drove one fist into the tall man's midriff and brought the other one up to his jaw.

They were terrific punches. They brought the sentence to an end, and they proved the efficiency of Sam Shay's simple but direct plan by bringing the man in the red sash to the ground, flat on his back, unmoving, arms lying loosely in the dirt beside him, eyes staring glassily at the tropical stars.

The blond girl had stopped at the thumping sound of the first punch. She came running back. She whispered excitedly: "It's in his left hip pocket. It's a piece of blue paper, folded."

Singapore Sam rolled his limp victim over on his face, and the girl swiftly explored the two hip pockets. She pulled out the blue paper, and Sam struck a match. The flaring light showed a carefully drawn section of a chart—a chart obviously traced from a larger chart. It was a corner of the loneliest spot in the eastern archipelagoes.

Before the flame died Sam had it fixed in his mind. It embraced a small part of the Molucca Sea, the northeastern tip of Celebes, and the northern islands in the Molucca group, including Morotai and smaller islands.

A ring in red crayon was drawn about one of these latter, and the island within the ring was labeled "Murder Island."

He was about to tell the girl that, though he had never visited Murder Island, he knew something about it, and that he intended to take their prisoner aboard his schooner and find out all he could about that remote and inaccessible speck on the map.

Before he could speak, the man he had knocked out was coming up from the ground and shaking his head as he did so. He held both hands stiffly out before him. He was making a strange noise that was half-whimper and half-growl. Sam could not see his face, he could see only the darkness where it was.

He aimed for that oval of darkness and swung his fist—and missed. The man came plunging at him, struck him in the chest with both hands and sent him tripping backward to fall into a bush. There was a sudden small scream from Miss Bondy, then the crackling sound of paper being crumpled. She cried: "Get him, Sam!"

The man in the red sash was running, streaking it across the Reclamation ground in the general direction of Brah Basah Road. Sam might have overtaken him if there hadn't been another development.

Two figures were approaching Sam and Miss Bondy from different directions. Sam caught a glimpse of red cotton in a ray from a far-away light. Red turbans meant Sikh policemen!

"Halt!" said one of them.

"Halt or I fire!" said another, quite in the best colonial police tradition.

The beams of pocket torches fanned about and found the red-headed man in the path. The two Sikh policemen, with revolvers drawn, closed in.

They were very polite. Politeness is one of the remarkable things about a Sikh policeman. Another is firmness. Another, perhaps, is memory.

Marthana Bondy proved what a clever young lady she was. She began a bright explanation of everything. She and this gentleman, she explained, had been walking in the park when they were set upon by footpads.

She might have gotten away with it if one of the policemen hadn't chanced to recognize Sam Shay.

"Ah!" he said genially. "It is Singapore Sammy Shay!"

There was something about the way he said it that made Marthana stop explaining. While one of the tall and polite policemen held his gun on the suspicious pair, the other frisked Sam and found Marthana's little automatic pistol.

That was serious. Bringing small arms ashore in Singapore, or having them in your possession without proper authority, is no small crime. But being Captain Sam Shay was almost as serious a crime.

The two criminals, or the criminal and his beautiful accomplice, were forthwith marched to Beach Road. One of the Sikhs stopped two double rickshaws. One of the Sikhs drove to the police station with Miss Bondy in one of them, the other Sikh rode with Sam Shay in the other.

SINGAPORE SAM WAS booked on a charge of carrying a concealed firearm without a permit, and was locked in a cell. Miss Bondy was permitted to use a telephone. She was permitted to visit his cell presently, and she was furious.

"And I can't do anything about their stupidity!" she stormed. "But I can and will get you out of here in a hurry! If you're here longer than an hour, it'll be because the Baxton Corporation has lost its political pull! Did you see enough of that chart to know what it's about?"

"Yes. The place ringed was Murder Island. It's in the Moluccas. It's an old pearling station. It was fished out years ago. The British had a station there. That's pretty wild territory."

"Cannibals?"

"I don't know. It's a long way from where Ray Baxton vanished."

"Why is it called Murder Island?"

"Long before the days of the mutiny on the Bounty pirates settled there, they say. They all murdered each other. That's the commonest story. It's been called Murder Island for centuries."

"And we'll probably all be murdered here," Marthana said grimly. "I'm awfully glad you're going to take charge of this mess, Sam. You're a real comfort to a girl. Listen: when they let you out, go to Raffles and register. Then what?"

"I want that bird in the red sash."

"Will you look in at Raffles occasionally in case I need you in a hurry? If I can't come, I'll send a message as soon as possible. I want to contact Ben Rosen and see what he wants to do next."

"Okay."

She went. Less than an hour later she demonstrated that the Baxton Corporation was not without political pull in Singapore. Sam was released. He was not only released; he was informed by a suave young man in white linen that he was to be permitted the freedom of Singapore for forty-eight hours.

"You mean," Sam said skeptically, "I won't be arrested again?"

"You will not be molested again in any way."

As Sam was leaving the jail, a panting Chinese coolie accosted him. Sam thought at first he was a beggar, but he stopped when the coolie panted:

"Masta! You allatime that Capum Shay?"

"That's right. What wanchee?"

The coolie gasped for breath. He had evidently been running hard.

"That Mistla Pound, him velly sick! Him hab got that velly big fight! That Mistla Pound, him dlink velly much, makee much bhobbery, makee much fight!"

"Where?"

"Yen Gow's! You come 'long chop-chop?"

"Yep."

Rufe had evidently not taken his advice, and was roaring

drunk. And when Rufe started a fight, cracked skulls and worse were apt to result.

The China boy scuttled, and Sam followed. A rickshaw was waiting at the curb before the jail. The owner of the *Blue Goose* climbed aboard, the rickshaw boy picked up the shafts and started off at a trot, and the messenger, grasping the back of the vehicle, trotted along and theoretically pushed.

Yen Gow's was a joint even more disreputable than Hop Fang's—a dispensary of booze, gambling, smoke and lower vices; a hangout for sailors of all nationalities, of thugs, footpads, pickpockets and the kind of women who consort with such.

The rickshaw rolled smoothly up Beach Road to Tan Quee Street, turned sharply right after two blocks, and entered an alley. Sam Shay, puffing at a cigarette, did not question this maneuver. Tan Quee Street was packed with children of night, and it was slow going. The alley was a short cut.

It was a lonely, dark and deserted alley, but at one point there was considerable activity. Needle rays of light from shuttered windows told an old, old story. Some helpless wayfarer was being held up or slaughtered.

One needle ray flicked along the wicked curve of a scimitar in the hands of a Nubian who was nothing but flashing eyes, flashing teeth and soiled white breechclout. There occurred, from darkness, the scream of a strangling man. That would be the victim, at present immersed in a pool of intense blackness.

As the scimitar started on its downward swing, the rickshaw pulled abreast. Sam Shay dived overboard. He clipped

the black man on the side of the head and reached down
for the scimitar's handle. It clattered to muddy cobble-
stones.

He heard his rickshaw go scuttling away, as rickshaws
have a way of doing under such circumstances, and the
receding asthmatic wheezing of the China boy, too. He
had the scene and the fight to himself.

Only there was no fight. One blow of his fist had turned
the tide, it appeared, and the enemy was in flight, too. He
saw blacker shadows than the shadow in which he stood—
black and shiny shadows, flitting off down the alley.

He struck a match, and its light fell on a fat, horrified
little man who cowered against bright satin cushions in a
sedan chair. The sputtering flame picked out blood-red,
canary-yellow, sapphire-blue and emerald-green. And the
turban wound about the fat little head was of white satin.

Here was a personage.

5

"ALL YOURS!"

THE MATCH FLAME steadied and found other splendor. The personage appeared to be swathed in satin robes of dyes stolen from a rainbow—sea-blue and magenta and purple, and there was a golden girdle about the personage's middle.

He puffed and wheezed and his little ratty eyes stared up at the flushed face of the red-headed man. He wheezed, "Help me out, pliz."

Sam Shay took him by the elbows and hoisted him out of the chair and stood him on his feet. He was shorter and fatter than Sam Shay had guessed—and richly perfumed. The perfume reminded Sam of a dark-eyed woman with thick black hair, a woman in Rangoon who was called The Spider.

Under the perfume was the sickly faint breath of opium. The rescued was probably a small-time sultan. There were no more decadent men in the world than these little sultans.

Sam Shay looked at that shuddering, horrified little man whose fat neck had been within a split second of being cut by a scimitar in the hands of a starving Nubian, and said, "Brother, you need a drink—bad."

The scented stranger in satin chattered: "My life is in your hands. My kingdom is at your disposal. Anything that I possess is yours. I am the Sultan Renna Chad Maggore of Saballa. You have snatched my life from the jaws of death, and I will repay you to the last farthing."

Sam was familiar with Saballa. It was a small island off the northern coast of Borneo, a tropical paradise once noted for its water diamonds, but now specializing in copra and palm seeds. Saballa was a British protectorate.

He took the Sultan Renna Chad Maggore of Saballa firmly by the arm and escorted the trembling little monarch to Rochore Road. On the way, the Sultan acquired Sam's name and his Singapore address—Raffles Hotel.

"I will reward you fittingly, my friend."

"Forget it," Sam said amiably.

A British police officer, in white, distinguished by his black Sam Browne belt, saw them as they entered the brightly lighted street. He gave Sam a cynical smile and said, "Pleasant evening, isn't it, Captain Shay?" And Sam guessed that word had gone out that he actually was to be permitted the freedom of the city for forty-eight hours.

The policeman asked questions and produced a notebook and pencil. Sultan Renna Chad Maggore answered fluently and with indignation. It was an outrage and a scandal that a man of his importance should be set upon by black thugs practically in the heart of the city of Singapore—England's boasted gem of the southern Orient!

The policeman made copious notes, promised to send the chair to his residence and called a rickshaw.

The Sultan of Saballa begged Sam to accompany him home, an invitation which the red-headed young man firmly declined. And the sultan departed, waving his fat, jeweled little hands and yelling his gratitude.

Sam secured another rickshaw and was taken to Yen Gow's. Rufe Pound wasn't there. Yen Gow swore he hadn't been there, and that there had been no fight of any description all evening. It was mysterious. Sam tried, in turn, the Brass Mermaid, the Glory Hole, and the Sapphire Lizard.

Here he found Rufe Pound playing stud poker with five other sailing men and drinking a rum swizzle. The mate of the *Blue Goose* looked comparatively sober. His eyes weren't bloodshot, and his face was its normal hue—a baked brick red. He saw Sam across the smoke-filled room, in the doorway, recognized him without delay, thereby proving he wasn't very drunk, and waved to him.

Sam went around behind his chair and noted that the mate's stack was low.

"Want me, skipper?"

"How long've you been here?" Sam asked.

"Ever since I left you at Hop Fang's. What's wrong?"

"Been in any scraps?"

"Me? I should say not! But I'm gonna be if that one-eyed guy deals many more aces to himself back to back!"

"I'll see you aboard," Sam said.

"Okay, skipper."

Sam went out. It was indeed mystifying. He concluded that the Chinese coolie who had accosted him outside the jail had intended to lure him into the trap into which the Sultan of Saballa had fallen. Why? Merely a simple robbery scheme?

He took a rickshaw to Raffles, registered, and inquired if there had been any word from Miss Bondy. There had not

been. He was shown to a room. This attended to, he went
out again and prowled up Beach Road to Brah Basah, up
Brah Basah to Princep Street, and across to Rochore. He
met several sailors he knew, and he asked them if they had
seen a tall, dark-haired man wearing a dark-red sash. They
had not. He put the same question to several shopkeepers
he knew, with the same result. He wandered down to the
water front, and questioned several pier watchmen, but no
one had seen the man in the dark-red sash.

SAM RETURNED TO Raffles, went into the bar and ordered
a whisky sour. He was sipping this amiable beverage when
a brown-skinned man in uniform came in, looking as if
he might have just stepped out of a musical comedy. The
uniform consisted of a bright red tunic, cream-colored
riding breeches and glossy black riding boots. He wore an
emerald-green cap of the Italian army type, with a high
crown and a long black patent leather vizor. He was about
five feet three inches tall.

"Mr. Zhay?" he asked, and clicked his heels smartly.

"Shay," Sammy said.

"I am Major Ram Singh, Mr. Zhay, in the service of his
majesty the Sultan Renna Chad Maggore of Saballa. I
come to present to you the compliments of his majesty and
to request that you accept a trifling token of his esteem"—
Major Ram Singh took another breath—"for your fearless-
ness and bravery in delivering his majesty from the hands
of black footpads at great personal risk."

Captain Shay grinned.

"His majesty, the Sultan Renna Chad Maggore of
Saballa, wishes to confer upon you the order of the Rising
Silver Star and the Fighting Caribou of Saballa. I am dele-

gated to pin this order upon your courageous breast with my own hands, sir."

"It was nothing," Sam Shay said.

Major Ram Singh drew himself up to his full height and attained an air of severity.

"It was nothing," he said indignantly, "to save the life of Renna Chad Maggore, the Sultan of all Saballa, the pearl in the lotus, the diamond in the beak of the flamingo?"

"I apologize," Sam said. "It will be an honor to receive this token of his majesty's friendship for the service I was fortunate enough to render him."

That was the kind of talk Major Ram Singh wanted. His shiny brown face was all smiles. His small black eyes sparkled.

"But not here," he said.

"Of course not, major. We'll go to my room. Okay?"

"Okay, sir, Mr. Zhay!"

They went to Sam's room, which was a spacious and airy room on the second floor, with a balcony of its own.

When the door was closed, Major Ram Singh removed from a pocket of that amazing uniform a small black box. It was of ebony inlaid with mother o' pearl. He opened the lid. Resting on red satin was a small silver-and-enamel ornament, with rays of silver representing the rays of a bright star, and with a green-enamel center on which, in browns and reds and blues, was a neat portrait of a caribou.

The little brown man placed the box on a table, and, standing at salute, said dramatically: "Mr. Zhay, it gives me great pleasure and great honor to confer upon you the order of the Rising Silver Star and the Fighting Caribou, to commemorate your services in saving the life of his royal majesty the Sultan Renna Chad Maggore, of Saballa, and I humbly request that you accept the undying gratitude of his majesty's loyal subjects! You will kindly kneel."

Singapore Sam knelt. When Major Ram Singh had pinned the medal on the breast of his jacket, Sam said: "Kindly convey to his majesty my gratitude for this great honor. I will treasure it to the grave."

He got up and bowed. Major Ram Singh bowed, with another clicking of heels.

"But that isn't all, sir, Mr. Zhay."

"What do you mean, this isn't all?"

"One moment, pliz!" He went to the hall door and threw it open with a dramatic flourish, A file of brown-skinned men came into the room, carrying objects. There must have been a dozen of them. Some carried teakwood or sandal-wood chests. Others carried bulky bundles.

With each article went a little speech from the major, all of it commemorating the fact that Captain Zhay had, single-handed and at great personal risk, saved the life of a fat little rascal in a white satin turban who smelled like a black-eyed woman in Rangoon.

It was mostly satins and silks and tapestry. Every time a box or bundle was opened, out popped another chunk of silk or satin as heavy as sail canvas and of some color from the wilder regions of the spectrum. There were also bronze incense pots, curry sets in lacquer and brass and several little cabinets intricately carved and inlaid.

There were no fistfuls of diamonds or emeralds or rubies or sapphires. Sizing it up with his experienced trader's eye, Captain Shay estimated tapestries and silks and satins and boxes of spices and curry sets at a total of less than two hundred dollars.

The fat little sultan was probably broke, reduced by the petering out of his water diamonds and the depression to a bare existence, yet he must show his gratitude to his red-headed savior. Touching and Oriental and pathetic.

"But that isn't all, sir, Mr. Zhay!" the little brown man cried. "I have saved the pearl, the choicest jewel of all, until the last!" His eyes sparkled and glowed. His white teeth flashed. And Sam Shay had a quick vision, in his mind, of a very fine and very large and pure water diamond.

Ram Singh threw open the door. A native girl of about sixteen walked in. She seemed to glide. She was a small girl with skin like golden satin. Her eyes were large and dark and sparkling. Her costume was a single length of pale-blue silk which was wound about her in a wide spiral from above her small, round breasts to her small sandaled feet.

Sam Shay noticed indifferently that she was pretty and that her figure was slim and alluring. He wasn't interested in her. He would have taken, perhaps, a more lively interest in her if he could have guessed what a strange and tragic part she would take in unraveling the mystery of Murder Island.

At that moment she was to Sam Shay nothing but a slim and sleek and beautiful young native girl. He wasn't interested in what she might have in her folded golden hand. He was anxious to get this flowery Oriental ritual over with. He wanted to look for the man in the red sash. He wanted to visit the yacht Victory and question her captain and wireless man.

The girl glided into the room with a grace that was

somewhat pantherlike. Her soft, blue-black hair rippled freely off her lovely small face.

"This!" the major cried.

Sam waited for the pretty little native girl to open her hand. She didn't open it.

"The sultan's beloved youngest daughter," Major Ram Singh went on—"the most priceless jewel of all! She is yours!"

"This girl?" Sam gasped.

"Yes!"

"Mine?"

"All yours, *tuan!*"

6

MURDER

SAM LOOKED AT the beloved youngest daughter of the Sultan of Saballa with sudden cold dismay. The beautiful dark eyes sparkled at him mischievously; the long, thick lashes swept down to her flushed cheeks, then leaped up, and the eyes were sparkling up at him again. The young lady was apparently not at all averse to being presented to him, so to speak, on a silver platter.

"I'm sorry, major," he said, "but I'm traveling light."

Major Ram Singh stared at him with astonishment. "You don't mean you are refusing her—this beautiful and joyous young creature?"

"I do, major. I live a hard life. It's no life for a girl."

"But she, too, has given her consent, Captain Zhay! She gives it freely. She has heard of you. You are like a god to her people!"

Sam looked with distress at the Princess of Saballa. "You'll have to go back to your father," he said.

The Princess of Saballa smiled at him radiantly. Her eyes glowed.

"She does not speak English," said the major.

"I'm sorry," Sam said to the girl, in Malay. "You will have to return to your father—with my regrets."

"She does not speak Malay, either," said the major. "She speaks nothing but Saballanese. And you cannot return her to her father. The sultan would be grossly insulted!"

"Major," Sam said firmly, "I'm sorry about this. You see, I'm an American. In America, we don't do this sort of thing."

"But you are not in America, sir, Mr. Zhay! And she is a gift. And you cannot return a gift in Saballa! The sultan would be furious. If you rejected a gift made with such goodness of heart, he might do anything! He might even order that you be poisoned!"

"I'll have to take the chance," Sam said.

The Princess of Saballa spoke. Her small red mouth opened and a small but imperious voice was heard. It rung clearly, like a good silver bell.

"She wants to know," the major translated, "why you do not welcome her to her new home with a large hug and a long kiss, as is the quaint American custom."

"Tell her the truth."

"I dare not, Captain Zhay! She is a creature of fire and lightning, passionate in love and fearful in hate! Her name is Koori. It is the name of a golden Saballa flower that blooms only in the full moon and sends forth a divine fragrance. You will learn to love her, I am sure. I must go now. Good night!"

"Hold on, major! You're taking her with you!"

Koori spoke again. More silvery words. This time the note of imperiousness was even more pronounced.

"She says," the major translated, "she has fallen in love with you on sight. She has carried your image in her heart since she was very small. You are her dream-god, *tuan*."

Again Koori filled the room with the tinkling of her sweet voice.

"She wants to know what is wrong with her."

"Nothing at all. She is perfect."

"She wants to know if it is her figure, which is the loveliest figure, with the softest grace, of any girl's figure on our island."

"You don't understand," Sam Shay protested. "She's wonderful. Her figure is beautiful. But I can't accept her."

He fidgeted. He wanted to continue his hunt for the man in the dark-red sash, and he was impatient to go aboard the Victory and begin asking questions. But he had lived in the Far East long enough to know that an interview of this nature isn't to be terminated abruptly.

The silvery voice spoke again, and Major Ram Singh grimly translated. "She wants to know if it is her face that you despise."

"Tell her she has the beauty of a freshly blossomed lotus, but I am too busy for a wife."

Koori sat down on the edge of Sam Shay's bed, tested the material of the pillow case with a thumb and forefinger, bounced up and down and spoke again.

"She says that this coarse stuff will never do for her red-haired god. I am to fetch sheets and pillowcases of finest white satin."

"You'd better break it to her," Sam Shay said resolutely, "that she isn't going to stay. Tell her I appreciate her, and that her loveliness is enough to drive a man to madness, but that she can't stay here. And tell the sultan he has been too generous. Get her out of here."

"*Tuan!*"

Koori stared at him long and searchingly. She spoke again.

"She is deeply insulted," said the major. "She is furious. The sultan will be even more furious. You have refused his most priceless gift! *Tinggal!*"

Koori preceded him through the doorway. She gave Sam Shay a look, as a parting glance, that was half-challenge and half-threat.

SAM SHAY CLOSED the door after them. He looked about the room, choked with gifts from the Sultan of Saballa. He picked up silks, satins and tapestries from the bed and hurled them into a corner.

His room smelled of sandalwood, gumwood, spice and the musky perfume Koori had used. Sam went out on his balcony and down a narrow stairway into the luxuriant tropical garden. He made his way to Beach Road and took up, once again, his search for the man in the red sash.

With time to think over the confusing mass of information Marthana Bondy had given him, he had formed several tentative opinions. One was that his old friend Jeff Carmichael might have been murdered in the wireless room of the yacht Victory on the night of April sixth and thrown overboard in connection with an elaborate plot to kidnap Ray Baxton, the drunken heir to the Baxton motor car empire. But Sam wasn't absolutely convinced that it was a kidnaping. He was sure on only one point: that the man in the red sash was representing the leaders of the conspiracy and could explain everything if he were properly persuaded. And Singapore Sam Shay was a master of the art of persuasion. It was still his plan to take the man in the red sash aboard the *Blue Goose* and employ such methods as might be necessary to encourage him to talk freely.

He spent more than an hour prowling about the water front and dropping into saloons and dives where he was known, making inquiries about the man in the red sash. His quest was no more successful than the former one had been.

When he returned to Raffles, there was a note for him at the desk from Marthana. He opened the sealed envelope and read:

Dear Sam:

Everything has blown wide open. Every reporter and secret service man in Malaya is hot on our trail. There is nothing we can do until we know more of what you are trying to find out for us. Ben Rosen says you are to use your own judgment. The sky is the limit on the money you have to spend in any connection. His only suggestion is that you have your schooner provisioned and ready for us to sneak aboard and away at a moment's notice. Mr. Rosen has wirelessed Captain Jayne to give you all possible assistance and to accept unquestioningly your advice and suggestions. With the hounds baying on our trails, we are absolutely helpless. I will get in touch with you somehow tomorrow. It is up to you to clear up everything and to get us secretly out of Malaya and to the island. I'm counting on you, Sam! Good luck!

Marthana.

Sam folded the note and placed it in his pocket. He would burn it up at the first chance. Thinking over its contents, he smiled a little grimly. "It is up to you to clear up everything and get us secretly out of Malaya and to the island!" That was a man's-size order. And with every reporter and spy in Singapore wanting to know where Ray Baxton was! He wished he could have a little talk with the beautiful Marthana?

The desk clerk said: "The young lady is waiting in your room, sir."

Sam went to his room. He threw open the door and went in, closing it firmly. Not until he was halfway across the room did he see the girl curled up asleep on his bed.

Sam Shay stopped so abruptly that he almost lost his balance. Without pausing, he executed an about-face and started to tiptoe toward the door. He had no further need for this room, and the Princess of Saballa was welcome to it!

But before he could reach the door, Koori was awake. She saw him and squealed with pleasure. He made a dash for the door, but the princess was off the bed and had overtaken him before his hand could reach the knob.

She threw her arms about his neck with another little squeal of joy and clung to him. She began babbling to him in her silvery tongue, laughing into his face, pressing herself close to him.

Sam didn't understand a word of it, but explanations were not necessary. She was his, and she was going to stay his! She was absolutely non-returnable!

With her hands clasped behind his neck, she held tight to him. Before he could avoid it, she kissed him. Then, when she saw his strained expression, she laughed. It was the laughter of a girl with a merry sense of humor, and there was no doubt that Sam Shay looked funny enough to be laughed at.

"Listen, sister—" he began.

She interrupted with more squeals and more bright silvery talk in the language of her island.

Someone knocked sharply at the door. Three sharp knocks. They were peremptory knocks—the kind of knocks that a visiting police officer might give to a door.

Koori stopped laughing. Her soft young arms slipped from his neck, and she looked up at him with enormous dark eyes, suddenly grave and questioning.

In that moment there had been another sound from the hall. In fact, a swift succession of sounds. There was a strange thud, then a long, hissing gasp, then a louder thud as if something had fallen to the floor. This was accompanied by a curious scratching sound along the door. Next, Sam heard swift soft footfalls receding down the hall. All this had occupied the space of not more than three seconds.

Sam strode to the door and opened it. A man lay face down on the floor with a dagger in his back, a dark-red sash about his waist!

7

"I WILL NOT FAIL."

EXCEPT FOR THE dead or dying man, the hall was empty. The killer had escaped.

The bone-and-brass-handled dagger had been placed where it was by an expert. And it had been driven in up to the hilt.

Sam Shay looked up and down the hall, bent down quickly, dragged the man in the red sash into the room, and shut the door. He glanced up at Koori. Her eyes were large and shocked. Her lips were faintly parted. She bent forward with her slim, golden arms crossed on her breast. She stared at the dead man. Her eyes flicked to Sam Shay. They remained steadily on his, dark and mystical and unfathomly Oriental.

He rolled the man over. The eyes were open, staring and already glazing. The man in the red sash was dead. The one man in Singapore who might have been of the slightest real use to Sam Shay in getting at the explanation of this baffling mystery had been stabbed in the back at Sam's very door.

He went through the dead man's pockets very thoroughly, but found nothing. He examined the knife and decided he wanted it. When he had worked it out, he took it into the bathroom, washed off the blood and examined it under the light over the basin.

The blade was about five inches long, and on it was stamped the name of its Hartford, Conn., manufacturer. And stamped into the bone handle were the initials OPQ.

He returned to the bedroom and walked out onto the balcony. The sky overhead was still black and starry, but there was a faint line of gray along the eastern horizon. As Singapore is almost on the equator, dawn comes there swiftly. There was no time to waste.

The body of the dead man must not be found in Sam Shay's room, or anywhere near his room. Putting the knife in his pocket for future reference, Sam dragged the dead man to the balcony, picked him up and carried him down the stairs into the garden. He carried the corpse the length of the garden and left it in a thicket of hibiscus bushes. Then he returned to his room.

Sam was a little worried about Koori. If she talked, she might get him into trouble. But that was a chance he would have to take. She was probably dumb. She would probably be afraid to talk. The motto learned by the children of these countries at an early age is, the less you say, the better luck you'll have.

When he returned from the garden, she was standing where she had been before. And when he went to the hall door, she spoke quickly in her silvery, soft tongue and pointed to the floor. There was a small spot of drying blood where she pointed. Not so dumb.

Sam removed it with a wet towel, made sure there was no other incriminating evidence, and opened the door. He stopped at the desk to pay for his room, told the clerk to give all the Oriental junk it contained to some charitable institution, and went out and put the Princess of Saballa into a double rickshaw.

Koori sat submissively beside him, with hands meekly folded in lap, but when he glanced at her, after he had given the rickshaw coolie directions, that mischievous sparkle had returned.

As the rickshaw stopped before the teakwood residence of the Sultan of Saballa, in its grove of banyan trees, Koori looked indignant. Sam jumped out, took her by the elbows and swung her to the ground.

He said amiably, "This is as far as you go, sister."

She surprised him by making no protest. She stood near a flame palm and watched him as he started back to the rickshaw.

But as he turned to the rickshaw again and hopped aboard, he felt decidedly uncomfortable. He had the uneasy feeling that he hadn't seen the last of the Princess of Saballa.

When the rickshaw vanished, she went briskly into the house.

The Sultan Renna Chad Maggore of Saballa was waiting for her in the room that he called his study. He was celebrating the dawn with a tall glass containing a mixture of Javanese *arrack* and French brandy.

In the language of their glamorous island, he said: "Well, my little pearl?"

He was displeased. His fat little face wore a pout.

"He brought me home," the loveliest and youngest of his daughters stated. "He will not have me."

"You are a dunce and a simpleton!" the sultan cried.

Koori smiled mischievously. "Fear not, my venerated father. The purpose of the arrow is to fly true to its mark. I will not fail."

8

THE VICTORY

SAM PAID OFF the rickshaw coolie at New Water pier, selected a sampan from the milling fleet of them and settled in the bow to think things over. The sun was climbing, and he had much to do.

The yacht Victory had changed her anchorage. She was anchored now in Keppel Harbor, and her snowy whiteness, her swift lines made of her a ship of dreams.

The redhead swung his eyes far to the left and picked up another ship, a hundred-foot schooner. Her hull was as blue as the sky. She rested like a blue gull on the glassy blue water. She was a dream ship, too. The handsomest and handiest sailing ship of her size in the archipelagoes. A two-master, with the masts well-raked, she was the design of a clever Scotsman who had intended her for the gun-running trade. The *Blue Goose* was the apple of Sam Shay's eye, and the salt of his existence.

Ah Fat, his Chinese cook, was the only man aboard. Rufe Pound, the first mate, and Willie Ru, the Malay *serang,* had not returned from a night probably given to riotous celebration.

While Ah Fat was making him a pot of coffee, Sam went below, showered, shaved and changed to fresh clothing.

Loud groans and profanity came through a porthole as he was slipping into a clean white coat. He recognized the voice as his first mate's and went above.

Rufe Pound was just coming aboard. One of his eyes was black, and there was a long and freely bleeding gash in his left cheek that would probably leave a very interesting scar. All of his pockets were inside out—protruding like rabbits' ears.

The mate was still drunk. His clothing was torn and filthy. He looked as if he had done most of his fighting last night on his back in a gutter. He came staggering aboard, groaning and cursing, but he sobered considerably when he saw Sam.

Sam paid off the sampan boy and said to Ah Fat: "Stick him under the cold shower, give him a shot of black coffee, then put him to bed and I'll sew him up."

Ah Fat took the big man below. Sam heard the hissing of the shower, then the bellows of Rufe as the cold water struck him. Ah Fat called Sam a few minutes later. He went below. The mate was swathed in a big bathrobe, drinking black coffee. When Sam had finished sewing up the cut in the big man's face, Rufe Pound was sober.

"We're checkin' out," Sam said.

"What's wrong?"

Sam had found that Rufe Pound retained dangerous information about as well as a sieve retains water. Slow, stupid, pig-eyed, enormous, Rufe Pound worshipped him, but he had one grave fault: he couldn't be trusted with secret information.

Sam said merely: "There seems to be some trouble brewing. It's safer to clear out."

"Okay. But we ought to go into drydock, skipper. We need all new running rigging, and the beard on her bottom's a yard long."

"It'll have to wait. We'll careen her at the first chance."

"Are we gonna lay here?"

"We'll kick over to Keppel Harbor to take on supplies. I'll tie up at Sheer's Wharf, but there's no more shore leave."

"Okay, skipper. I hope it ain't my fault."

"It's nobody's fault."

"How about that monkey business we saw on the beach—that guy with the phony smallpox?"

"Did you mention it to any one?"

"Not me!"

"Don't. It's dynamite."

"Is that what you're workin' on?"

"That's part of it."

Sam started the auxiliary, pulled the hook out of the mud and took the schooner around to Sheer's Wharf. He gave Ah Fat orders for supplies, then got into the dinghy and rowed out to the Victory which lay at anchor about a thousand feet from Sheer's.

There was antlike activity aboard the finest yacht afloat. Some of the crew were painting, others were holystoning decks, scrubbing down white enameled surfaces with sujee, still others were polishing brightwork. Two men with rifles were slowly pacing the deck.

One of these came to the ladder as Sam pulled alongside the little platform.

"No one's allowed aboard this ship."

"Tell Captain Jayne," Sam said, "that the man Mr. Rosen mentioned wants to talk to him."

Sam had no warning of the attack.

"Wait where you are." The deckhand went away. He returned in a moment and said curtly, "What's your name?"

"Captain Sam Shay of the *Blue Goose*."

"All right. Come aboard."

Sam made the painter fast and went aboard. Members of the crew, at their work, stared at Sam sullenly. They looked like men with grievances. There was mutiny in the air. Thinking of Ben Rosen's elaborate pains to hoax this crew, Sam reflected that the ways of deception are apt to end in tangles.

The man with the rifle escorted Sam forward and up to the boatdeck and to a door over which was riveted a brightly polished brass plate bearing the inscription, *Master.*

"In there, captain."

SAM PUSHED OPEN a screen door and went in. It was a

spacious and luxurious room. Not even on passenger liners
had he ever seen such luxurious quarters for a skipper. The
decorative note was decidedly modernistic, with chromium
inlaid in stripes in the hand-rubbed walnut walls, and with
chairs of chromium and bright-blue leather. It was like a
suite in a fashionable apartment hotel.

A man sat at a walnut-and-chromium desk. He wore
pink pajamas. He was a plump little man, with a pink,
round face, bulging blue eyes, a small blond mustache.
There were circles under his eyes, and his features other-
wise showed the marks of worry and suffering.

He did not get up or smile when Sam entered the room.
He merely stared at him with an expression of pop-eyed
surprise, as if he had expected someone entirely different.
He ran his eyes from Singapore Sam's untrammeled red
hair to his broad powerful shoulders and on down to his
white oxfords.

"Are you Captain Shay?" he asked in an unhappy voice.

"Yep."

"Well, sit down, captain. Has Mr. Rosen told you much?"

"Miss Bondy told me everything."

Captain Jayne looked even unhappier. He had evidently
been finishing breakfast. A large silver tray contained
delicate chinaware and silver utensils. He poured himself
another cup of coffee, sugared and creamed it and stirred
the mixture thoughtfully. It did not seem to occur to him
that his visitor might be in need of coffee or breakfast.

"Do you," Captain Jayne asked querulously, "feel that
you're quite—uh—competent to handle this situation?"

"No," Sam said firmly. "Do you?"

The pale blue eyes bulged a little more. And Singapore

Sam decided to stop wasting time on this worried, pompous little man. He was perfectly aware that Captain Jayne
was not above possible suspicion. If Ray Baxton had been
kidnaped, more than one man aboard must have been in
the plot. If successful, such a plot would reap fatter profits
than any kidnaping in history—millions! Captain Jayne
was logically open to suspicion.

"I noticed," Sam said, "you aren't flying anything yellow
at your masthead."

Captain Jayne put down the coffee cup with a clatter,
and gasped: "Did she tell you about that, too?"

"She told me everything. Jeff Carmichael was one of
my best friends. Do you know what will happen to you,
captain, if the word gets to official ears that you came in
here with a smallpox case and sent him ashore before you
went through quarantine?"

The yacht captain went suddenly white. Beads of sweat
suddenly appeared on his forehead. He said with unexpected passion: "Good God, of course I know! They'll have
my papers! It's a penal offense!"

"How about this crew? The trick was pulled off to fool
them—to make them think Ray Baxton was still aboard.
How long do you think you can keep them bottled up?"

Captain Jayne jumped out of his chair with as much
alacrity as if Sam had stuck a pin into him. His eyes seemed
to bulge more than ever.

"It's worrying me sick!" he bleated.

"Your crew doesn't look very happy," the red-headed
man said. "What are your plans?"

"What did Mr. Rosen suggest?"

"Nothing. What did he say in that message?"

"That you were to take complete charge of the situation, captain." It must have pained the pompous little man to say that.

"What," Singapore Sam wanted to know, "are you going to do about this crew?"

"I don't know!" Captain Jayne groaned. "I've told them there's to be no shore leave. I've checked the damage in the engine room, and the chief engineer says it will take a month to get the necessary parts from the States, and to fix both engines. It isn't a drydock job, but how can I keep these men penned up on this ship? They'll murder me! And if one of them slips ashore with that smallpox story, I'll be up before the British admiralty before you can drop a hat!"

"One of them did slip ashore," Sam pointed out. "That oiler."

"He won't talk. I've sent out orders for his arrest. He'll be clapped in jail the moment they find him. How about these others?"

"Tell them," Sam decided, "that Ben Rosen has authorized you to offer each man a bonus of five thousand dollars, payable on this ship's return to the port of embarkation— that's Frisco, isn't it?—for keeping their mouths shut. Put it up to them. It's up to them all to see that none of them blabs. Every one of them will police every other one."

CAPTAIN JAYNE LOOKED immensely relieved. He mopped his perspiring face with a breakfast napkin.

He muttered: "I'm very grateful to you, Captain Shay, for taking this interest in our troubles."

"I'm not taking any more interest in your troubles than I can help," the red-headed young man said vigorously. "I'm interested in nothing but the murder of my old friend Jeff

Carmichael. If I have to go through hell and high water to find out who killed him, and why, I'll do it. Everything else is incidental. So suppose we start with that. Who killed Jeff Carmichael and why?"

Captain Jayne looked resentful. His pale blue eyes bulged.

"All I know," he sputtered, "is that he was missing from the radio room the same night Ray Baxton disappeared. Miss Bondy can tell you more about it than I can."

"What are your theories?" When the yacht captain hesitated, Singapore said urgently, "Do you think it was a kidnap plot?"

Captain Jayne nodded firmly. "I certainly do. I don't believe Ben Rosen saw Ray Baxton go alone into that launch. I think Ben Rosen was too drunk to see anything. If Ray Baxton wasn't kidnaped, why was Carmichael killed and thrown overboard and why did that oiler cripple the engine?"

"If somebody ganged up on Ray Baxton that night and took him off this ship, why aren't some of your crew missing?"

"There might have been stowaways," Captain Jayne suggested.

"Unlikely," Sam said. "The story Ben Rosen tells is phony. Or it sounds phony. Every part of it sounds phony. Did a single member of your crew see any of it?"

"No, Captain Shay."

"Where were the stewards? Where was the deck crew? Where was the watchman?"

"They have all been accounted for," was the answer.

Captain Jayne's bulging blue eyes, his fat red face

disclosed nothing suspicious, but Sam remained suspicious. He saw that there was nothing to gain from questioning this pompous little yacht skipper, so he said: "I want to talk to the radio man. What's his name?"

"Claude Price. You'll find him in the radio room. I told him to stand by for you."

Sam went aft to the radio room. A skinny young man with wavy, silky blond hair was seated at the radio table with earphones on. He took them off when Sam came into the doorway, and jumped up. His face was long, bony and pale, and his eyes were sickly gray. He was an unhealthy-looking young man of twenty-three or four, nervous and jumpy, and he looked as if he hadn't slept much lately.

He grinned nervously.

"I'm Sam Shay," the red-headed young man introduced himself. "I guess you must be Claude Price."

The wireless operator said eagerly: "Oh, yes. I know about you. Jeff used to talk about you by the hour. It was horrible about Jeff, wasn't it? He was the finest fellow I ever knew."

"Yes," Sam said. "He was the finest fellow that ever lived."

There was a photograph of Jeff on the wall: a lean, hard face; black hair, black eyes, a large, smiling mouth. It was a good photograph; it showed Jeff as he was: honest and hard and amiable.

"Who killed him?" Sam asked.

"If I knew the answer to that," the radio man cried, "do you suppose I'd have been doing nothing all this time? God only knows who or why. I haven't been able to sleep since it happened."

"You were asleep *when* it happened."

"Yes. Miss Bondy came down just as I was getting dressed to go on duty. I said I hadn't seen Jeff. Then she went off looking again and found some spots of blood on the deck, there, and some on the rail, too. He must have been stabbed."

"Do you suspect anybody on board?"

"No, Captain Shay. I mean, not anybody in particular. I've been watching them all. Of course, there isn't a man aboard who mightn't have been in the plot, if it was a plot. Though for the life of me I can't see why anybody should scheme to kill Jeff. It just doesn't make sense."

Sam looked at him curiously. The sickly, slate-colored eyes met his unflinchingly. Sam formed the opinion, in a few seconds, that Claude Price was innocent of any part in the mystery of Jeff's murder and Ray Baxton's disappearance.

The wireless man said earnestly, "If there's anything I can do—"

"I'll let you know if there is. What's the chief's name?"

"Quigley."

"What?"

"Quigley."

"Is his first name Oscar?"

"No. Olaf."

"Is his middle initial P?"

"Yes. For Peterson, I think. Why?"

"Was he ashore last night?"

"I don't think so. Why?"

Sam dropped his hand into his coat pocket where the sheath knife was. "I just want to see him."

9

1,000 TO 1

WALKING AFT, SINGAPORE reflected that he wanted answers to six questions:

1. Why was Jeff Carmichael murdered and who murdered him?
2. Was Ray Baxton kidnaped, or did he leave in the launch as Ben Rosen said, or was he murdered and chucked overboard?
3. Why was the engine partially crippled that night?
4. Why was the engine totally crippled when the Victory entered Singapore harbor?
5. Why was the man in the red sash killed at the door of Sam's hotel bedroom?
6. Just what was the tie-up, if any, between Bruno Reddy, the oiler, and Ben Rosen?

Sam would like to have answers to other questions, too, but if these six were answered he would be temporarily satisfied.

He found the entrance to the engine room, and went down into an atmosphere of shining steel. Several men were at work dismantling the starboard engine. The chief engineer was bossing this gang. He was a gray-haired man in the late forties with the gnarled and scarred hands of a man who has spent a lifetime working with heavy machinery. He was softly cursing.

Sam introduced himself and said: "I'm curious about this oiler who skipped."

The chief was willing to talk. He said that all he wanted in life was to lay his hands on Bruno Reddy. He wanted to twist his head off with his bare hands, he wanted to disembowel him with a cold chisel, he wanted to chop him up into fine pieces and feed these pieces to garbage sharks and squid.

"Anybody mean enough to cripple up a fine piece of machinery like this deserves to be keel-hauled and spread-eagled! On top of that, he stole several of my personal belongings among which was a very fine sheath knife my oldest boy gave me last Christmas and a pipe and—"

"A sheath knife?"

"Sure. A fine sheath knife!"

"Would this be yours?" Sam took out of his pocket the sheath knife he had found embedded in the back of the dead man.

Olaf P. Quigley stared at it and yelled: "Well, by gosh and by golly! Sure it's mine! Where'd you find it?"

"Outside my door at Raffles this morning."

The chief looked puzzled. "What was it doin' outside your door?"

"That's what I want to find out—I'm trying to track this fellow down."

"If you track him down, all I ask is, hold him till I git there!"

"What does he look like?"

"He's a black-lookin' feller—black hair and black eyes and a real dark skin. Come up to my cabin. I got a snapshot of him somewhere."

They went to the chief's cabin. He rummaged about in his desk and presently found a snapshot, a fairly good close-up of a man whose age was about thirty—a scowling, heavy-featured man, with thick lips and defiant eyes.

"Can I have this?"

"Sure!"

"Can I keep the knife a while? I'll send it out when I'm through with it."

"Don't send it back, mister, till you've twisted it around inside him good!"

They returned to the engine-room, where Mr. Quigley explained in technical detail the damage Bruno Reddy had done. Sam inspected the port thrust bearing and the starboard engine, then returned to his dinghy and rowed back to the *Blue Goose.*

He was sure that Ray Baxton, the legal heir to that tremendous estate, had been murdered and thrown overboard on the night of the sixth, or had been kidnaped, or had somehow and for mysterious reasons escaped from the ship in that lost launch. He shook his head. In other words, he wasn't sure of anything. It was a confusion. It was a mess in which an innocent bystander was apt to be hurt.

AS HE PULLED the dinghy alongside the schooner and made fast, Ah Fat came waddling down the dock, puffing, red-faced, obviously in a state of perturbation.

And as Sam swung aboard, the cook came puffing and panting aboard. The Chinese yelled angrily: "No good! No can catchum! My tly! No luck."

"You tried what?"

"My tly catchum supplies," the cook panted. "No catchum. Velly funny."

"Why not?"

"No sellum. Velly funny."

"Who no sellum?"

"Nobody no sellum. I tly. No luck. Velly funny."

"You mean," Sam said, "they won't sell you supplies?"

"That's light. No sellum."

"But why the hell not? Isn't our money any good?"

"No savvee. Money plenty good. My tly. No can do. I tly fi'-six places. Allasame. Allasame like shuttee shop. No catchum supplies. No wanchee business. Velly funny pidgin."

"Well, it certainly is funny."

Something was happening. One of those strange things was happening. Sam wanted to feel it didn't make sense, but it made plenty of sense.

"You go up to Jardine's, Ah Fat. You talkee that Mr. Consadine. You tellee him I sent you. Savvee? You talkee him we wanchee supplies chop-chop."

The cook said wearily: "My tly. That Massa Consadine say no can do. Say velly solly. Say velly too bad, but no can sellum. Velly funny pidgin."

"All right, Ah Fat. Maskee."

Muttering, Ah Fat went forward. Near the mainmast he stopped, turned and yelled, "No catchum supplies—no chow! What thing can? We makee sclam, anyway?"

"I don't know, Ah Fat. Maybe we scram, and maybe we stay right here till hell freezes."

Sam went below. He looked into his first mate's cabin.

Rufe Pound was asleep on his back, snoring. Sam opened the door of his own cabin, but stopped at the threshold. A man was seated at his desk looking through papers. He had black hair and wide shoulders. His hair was clipped so short that Sam could see the scalp shining through. He wore white linen.

When he turned and looked up, one eye was slightly squinted. In the other was a monocle. He was about thirty-five years old and he looked, with his haircut and his full red mouth, like a German. He looked as if he might be a German army officer.

He said, without accent: "You're Captain Shay?"

"Yeah," Singapore drawled.

"They call you Singapore Sam?"

"Right again, mister."

"I hope you don't mind my looking through your papers."

"Not at all," Sam said dryly. "Help yourself. They're nothing but my private papers, and this is nothing but my private cabin. Aside from that, I personally own this ship. So that you might almost say you're on public property."

The man with the monocle did nothing about the red-headed man's tone of threat. He did not smile or apologize. He stared at him thoughtfully through the monocle.

"Then you don't mind?"

"Well," Singapore drawled, "what do you think?"

Nothing but a feeling that the man with the monocle was more than merely physically dangerous kept his fists inactive.

"Personally or officially?"

"So," Sam said, controlling himself, "it's an official visit?"

"Personally," the stranger blandly answered, "I think

you're a fascinating fellow. Officially, I think you're sawing yourself off almost as much trouble as, say, Kaiser Wilhelm did in 1914."

"Not from what you found there."

"Oh, no. I'd hoped, for your sake, captain, to find your clearance papers here. I happen to know that the Maharaja of Jarrib has a lot of pearl shells that he is most anxious to ship off to Sydney at a very decent rate."

"Jarrib?"

"You know Jarrib, don't you?"

"Yes, I know Jarrib very well."

"You'll get your clearance at once?"

"I'll think about it."

THE MAN WITH the monocle stood up. "I don't suppose," he said softly, "you care to tell me where Ray Baxton is."

"A fair question," Sam replied, "deserves a fair answer. Why won't the provision dealers sell supplies to my ship?"

A blue eye solemnly regarded him through a disc of glass.

"I want to clear," Sam went on. "Jarrib will do. Anywhere will do. But how can I clear unless I'm fitted out?"

The man with the monocle looked puzzled. He shrugged. "I don't know anything about that."

"Get off my ship," Sam said. "My knuckles are beginning to itch again."

The stranger picked up his sun helmet from the bunk, adjusted his monocle, stared at Sam cynically for a moment and walked out of the door, up the stairs, off the ship and out of Sam's life.

Singapore Sam was puzzled and more worried than he wanted to admit. He went on deck. His worries were confirmed by a man on the dock. The man was about seven feet tall and dressed in the regulation uniform of the Colonials, and he carried a rifle with bayonet attached.

"Captain Shay?"

"Yep."

The Colonial recited in a sing-song: "The executive secretary of Sir Henry Mallinson has issued orders that this ship is not to leave this wharf without official release. I am to stay aboard and see that the order is carried out."

"Okay, brother. Come aboard and make yourself cozy. This isn't a ship, anyway. It's a public park. Try that chair in the shade."

He recalled what Marthana Bondy had said in her note: "It is up to you to clear up everything and to get us secretly out of Malaya and to the island!" Looking at the soldier and thinking of the man with the monocle, he grinned.

The lid had blown off. The richest young man in the world had been reported coming to Singapore, and he hadn't yet been seen. It was as if a treasure ship that had set sail for a port was long overdue. The newspapers, the authorities, were curious. They would grow more curious. Marthana and Ben Rosen and Dr. Hobb were holed up somewhere, hiding from the hurricane of curiosity.

And Singapore Sammy's job was to provision his ship, get Marthana and the two men secretly aboard—and clear out! The odds were possibly 1,000 to 1 against his success. But he had to succeed. He had to go to Murder Island. Only by going to Murder Island, he was now sure, would he track down those responsible for the killing of Jeff Carmichael. And he was going to track them down. The man responsible for Jeff Carmichael's death was going to be killed with Singapore Sammy's bare hands. Not with weapons, but with his bare hands.

A Chinese coolie came trotting down the dock with something white in his hand. It was addressed, in Marthana's crisp, firm handwriting, to Captain Sam Shay, schooner *Blue Goose,* Sheer's Wharf.

The note said:

> Dear Sammy:
>
> We are hiding on a rubber plantation about four miles out of Singapore. We will lie low until you come and take charge of us. It's the Westover plantation. We are at section ten bungalow. Use your judgment, but get us out of town as soon as you can. The suspense is terrific. We are absolutely in your hands.
>
> Good luck, redhead!
>
> M.

Sam burned the note, as he had the other. The colonial, lounging under the after deck awning, was looking at him suspiciously. A fat man in white drill and a brown sun helmet was lounging on the dock, looking at him suspiciously.

Two tall, handsome young men came striding down the dock. Both were strangers. Both were dressed in fresh white drill. The sun helmets of both had the same pristine, snowy whiteness. They were similarly tanned and blue-eyed. Englishmen. Englishmen on official business.

Sam went to meet them.

"Captain Shay?" said one of them crisply.

"Yep."

"You are to come with us, please."

"Kindly put on a coat," said the other.

"Where are we going?" Sam asked. "To the residency."

10

INQUISITION

MORE TROUBLE. VERY serious trouble. Sir Henry
Mallinson, the governor, wanted to see him. Sam put
on his coat and went up the dock between the two tall,
grim-looking young Englishmen to where, on Tanjong
Pagar Road, a Rolls-Royce touring car, with two *syces* in
the front seat, was waiting.

One of the Englishmen held open the door and bowed
stiffly. Sam got in. The two Englishmen got in and seated
themselves on either side of him.

The Rolls-Royce whizzed through Singapore, and the
red-headed man in the back seat knew he was in for trouble. He knew he was in for the kind of trouble that you can't
explain yourself out of. This was official trouble.

No doubt every move he had made since last night had
been watched and weighed and talked about—officially! It
was as if he had gone fishing for a sardine and had hooked a
whale. The whale wouldn't let go and he couldn't let go. The
heir to an industrial empire worth eight hundred million
was missing or murdered; at least, he had left behind a
whirling mystery, and Sam Shay was caught up into the
whirl.

It was like a war. Didn't he know that cables were ticking and wireless machines were flashing, that whole corps of men—a great human engine of investigation had been set into action!

Where was Ray Baxton?

Sam went into the residency accompanied by the two grim young Englishmen. He was taken into this palace and ushered down long, cool, dusky halls and through great rooms and into a large white room that seemed to be filled with men.

He recognized a gray-haired man with a flowing gray mustache as Sir Henry Mallinson. A thin, white-haired, red-faced man in white he recognized as the American Consul. The faces of others were familiar. One was a Eurasian spy. Another was a colonial secret service man. A square-faced man of sixty with bristling white hair was the chief of the Singapore police.

A flat, powerful voice said: "Captain Shay?"

That was Governor Mallinson.

"Yes, Sir Henry."

"You are the captain and owner of a trading schooner called the *Blue Goose?*"

"Yes sir."

"You spent the night in Raffles Hotel?"

"Yes, sir."

"You paid a visit to the yacht Victory this morning?"

"Yes, sir."

"Why, if I may ask?"

"Captain Jayne, in command of the Victory, is an old friend. I rowed out to say hello."

Every face registered skepticism.

"Are you aware that a man was killed in Raffles last night?"

"No, sir."

"Do you know anything about this killing?"

"No, sir."

Sir Henry Mallinson stared at Sam Shay coldly.

"Are you aware what the purpose of this questioning is, captain?"

"No, Sir Henry."

"Did you become acquainted with a blond young woman in Hop Fang's place yesterday evening?"

Sam hesitated. "I did, sir."

"Where did you go with her?"

"We took a drive and went for a short walk along Raffles Reclamation. We were arrested."

"Were you followed into the park by a man who wore a red sash, a white satin shirt and blue velvet trousers?"

"Not that I was aware of, Sir Henry."

"You didn't knock this man down in the park?"

"No, sir."

"Had you ever seen Miss Bondy previously?"

"Never."

"Have you seen her since?"

"No, sir."

THE AMERICAN CONSUL now took a hand. He said: "Captain Shay, we know you are lying. I brought your dossier along. You have been told repeatedly to stay away from Singapore. You are an inveterate trouble-maker. We know that your innocence is a pretense. We should not have called you here if we hadn't checked up on you thoroughly. You are simply refusing to be helpful."

Sam gazed at him pleasantly. "In what way, sir?"

"Talk! Tell us what you know! Do you think we're idiots?"

"I don't know what you mean."

"Very well. The man who was found murdered in the garden at Raffles this morning was the man who followed you and Miss Bondy into the park last night. Do you deny that you punched that man in the park?"

"I do."

"You're lying!"

"I don't know what you're talking about. I don't know anything about a murder. And I don't see what it's got to do with me."

A dozen pairs of eyes stared at Sam Shay with various expressions. There was doubt, there was skepticism, there was dark suspicion. There was no friendliness.

The chief of police said suddenly: "Where is Ray Baxton?"

Sam looked at him with vague eyes. "You mean, the son of Oliver Baxton?"

"You know what we mean!"

"I'm sorry, chief. I'm completely at sea."

The chief said: "I'll take him along, Sir Henry. I'll see if we can't make him talk." He said it with grimness. "Take him along, Judkins. You go too, Burroughs."

The two young men who had brought Singapore to the residency took him to the jail. He was locked in a cell, but not for long. He was taken into a dark, stuffy room with which he was not unfamiliar. Five grim-looking men, all strangers, fired questions at him.

Sam denied everything. He denied having knocked out the man in the park. He denied all knowledge of the same man's murder. He denied previous or later acquaintance with Marthana Bondy, and all knowledge of her present whereabouts.

Dr. Hobb and Ben Rosen were not mentioned. It was the evident intention of his inquisitors to tell him as little as possible. He learned that the wheels of an eight hundred million dollar industrial empire could grind exceeding fine.

It was dark when Sam was returned to his cell. He had been too busy to eat all day. He had had nothing to eat since yesterday noon. He was hungry and worried and hot.

A man appeared in the ill-lit corridor. He came lounging along, with a cigarette pasted to one corner of his lower lip. He exhaled a cloud of smoke into the cell and murmured, "A wise man would have taken it on the lam."

Sam was slow in recognizing that slim, shadowy face. He was conscious of mild shock. Always, it seemed to him, at such moments as this, this man appeared like a manifestation of the devil. He was supposed to be a newspaperman. He was known as Brain Fever Addison.

It was about all that Sam Shay knew about him. He had encountered Brain Fever Addison in strange places under strange circumstances. He was like a phantom. Just who he was and what he did Sam did not know and, for that matter, was destined never to learn. He materialized from shadows, and to shadows he always returned.

He began to talk in his strange way: "The only trouble with red-headed men is that they try to mix too much nitrogen with their glycerin. Now take me for example. Blond hair stands for childishness, red for violence and dark for maturity and balance. Blue-eyed people make good aviators, but brown-eyed don't. The blue pigment stands for recklessness, whether you're flying a plane or sailing a schooner. Now, me—I'm brown-haired and black-eyed."

"Nuts."

"When a rumor has a knife in it, the time, as I said before, has come to take it on the lam. Your reaction time is slow when the brain orders moderation. You're a bungling innocent, so I'm letting you go bye-bye. If I were you, redhead, I would marry Koori and settle down on some nice tropical island where there aren't any opportunities for trouble—and raise a large family. So long, lad."

Brain Fever Addison sauntered away, leaving behind the aroma of utter mystery. He might have been a disembodied ghost. He was the man who knew everything. Sam had encountered him, always in this queer way, in Indo-China, in Burma, in Java, and in various parts of the archipelago.

FIVE MINUTES AFTER his departure, a jailer came and unlocked Sam's cell and told him he was at liberty to go. It was impressive and awesome. It was as if Brain Fever Addison, that shadow of a man, was the most powerful man in the Far East. He had decided that Sam was innocent. So Sam was freed!

The Eurasian was waiting for Sam in the jail office.

"You can clear out now," he said. "And make it snappish!"

"Make it what?"

"Make it snappish!"

"Make it snappish?"

The Eurasian said insolently: "Am I telling you?"

"One of us is nuts."

The fact that Sam Shay had red hair began to make itself felt. He restrained the impulse to slap the Eurasian's nose.

He walked rapidly on. Brain Fever Addison had left no clear, useful ideas behind. His intention always seemed to be to cloud men's minds as a squid clouds the water about him. Yet Sam gleaned that he was to pursue his business, once again, with a strange kind of official approval.

Night had fallen. Outside the jail he met his first difficulty. He was fairly mobbed by newspapermen. There were upwards of two dozen of them, all of whom had apparently been tipped off that Singapore Sam Shay was the only known focal point of the Baxton mystery.

A dozen voices at once asked him the question bluntly: "What do you know about Ray Baxton?"

"Nothing."

"Where is he?"

"I don't know."

"Is he in Singapore?"

"Same answer."

He was a little appalled at their ferocity. He had never been the object of this kind of attention before. He kept his temper as they crowded him and jostled. He kept his temper even when they poked him and grew angry and yelped at him.

He broke through them finally, jumped into a passing rickshaw and yelled at the coolie to run all the way to Sheer's Wharf. He was followed. He had expected to be followed. He knew that everything he did from now on would be watched with great suspicion. He suspected that he had been freed to go about his business, so the authorities could spy out just what his business was.

There were more newspapermen at the dock, lounging

about, and Sam knew that among the crowd were spies also.

It was discouraging. How could he pursue his search for Bruno Reddy, the oiler, and make arrangements to bring Marthana Bondy, Ben Rosen and Dr. Hobb secretly aboard?

He had only one thing to be thankful for—the night was moonless. The stars were bright, but there was no moon.

He went aboard. The sentry was gone. Jardine's supply boat was alongside, and coolies were carrying crates and boxes of provisions aboard. Ah Fat was on the after deck, supervising.

"I thought you told me," Sam said, "nobody sellum supplies."

The Chinese cook shrugged his fat shoulders. "Me no savvee. Velly funny pidgin. Evelybody allatime no sellum supplies. Nobody wanchee my money. Bye-bye—chop-chop evelybody wanchee sellum! When we makee sclam?"

"Soon."

"Too soon allatime not soon enough. That missy go 'long?"

"What missy?"

"That plitty litty missy downside that cabin?"

"My cabin?"

The fat Chinese cook was laughing. "Hai! You pay look-see. You allatime like. Hot dog!"

Sam went below. Rufe Pound and Willie Ru, the Malay *serang*, were in Rufe's room, sitting at a table with a squat black bottle and two glasses between them.

Rufe cried happily: "Hi, skipper! Who's the tomato?"

"What tomato?"

"In your cabin, skipper. Oh, my. Oh, goodness. Give a look. If you don't want her, can I have her?"

Sam went down the corridor and opened his door. A girl with shining blue-black hair was seated on the edge of his bunk, bouncing up and down, with small golden sandals hobbling on the tips of her little golden feet.

"*Koori!*"

11

LITTLE-ARROW

THE PRINCESS OF Saballa clapped her hands, squealed and jumped up. Before Singapore Sammy could retreat, she had bounced off the bunk and had flown to him with her arms outstretched. He tried to sidestep that laughing, squealing onslaught, but he was again too slow. With rapturous little gurgles, she jumped up and wrapped his head in her arms, and she clung to him with a ferocity that dismayed him.

His nose was pressed into her warm, scented neck. Koori laughed and hung on.

Sam grabbed each of the small, golden hands and forcibly began to free himself, when the voice of Rufe behind him said, "When did this happen?"

"It didn't happen," the red-headed man sputtered.

"Well," the mate said judiciously, "it looks to me like it happened plenty. Where did you buy her, boss?"

"I didn't buy her. She was a gift."

"Boy! If it was raining diamonds, you'd be caught out with a shovel and a gunnysack! Is this hers?" He indicated a small and handsome rosewood chest inlaid with mother o' pearl.

"I guess so."

"Who was sap enough to give her away?"

Sam explained the circumstances of his acquisition of the Princess of Saballa, and of the strenuous efforts he had made to return the gift.

"You mean," Rufe said with astonishment, "you ain't gonna keep her?"

"No."

"Okay. I'll take her."

He reached for Koori. She darted behind Sam, placed her arms about his waist and clung there. She had apparently learned one word of English. She used it now seven times. "No, no, no, no, no, no, no!"

"She speaks English!" Rufe said delightedly. "Well, I always did like my women to show a little resistance. We'll just stow that chest in my cabin."

"No," Sam said. "Come on, sweetheart."

He took Koori by the hand. "Back where I come from," Rufe said, "people don't look close at gift horses. They just show they're glad. What are you gonna do with her?"

"Take her back to her old man again."

"Boss, you ain't human. I thought you told Ah Fat we was checkin' out chop-chop."

"We are."

"We better. There's been smart guys aboard all afternoon. Askin' questions. They had Willie Ru locked up in jail askin' him what did he know about the Victory. He just got out. What's goin' on, anyhow? Who are these guys, millin' around the dock? I'll bet a million bucks it all started with that phony smallpox business. Did it?"

"It did."

"Have you seen the clearance papers they sent?"

"I didn't ask for clearance papers,"

"Well, they sent some down, anyway. On your desk."

Sam glanced at the document. He had been given a clearance to San Francisco!

"The fellow who brought it," Rufe said, "told me to tell you to get to hell out of here."

"When was this?"

"Just a few minutes ago."

"Who was it?"

"That pin-headed punk from the consulate."

"Wallaby?"

"That's right—Wallaby."

Sam said grimly: "Check the water tanks. We'll clear tonight."

He took Koori's hand again and took her ashore, where they were promptly surrounded by newspapermen. Flashlights blazed in Sam's and Koori's faces. She clung to him in terror as he shouldered a way through the crowd and loaded her into a double rickshaw. There were more flashlights as the rickshaw started off. Koori cowered against him, covered her face with her hands and shivered with fright.

Several rickshaws followed them all the way to the residence of the Sultan of Saballa. Sam paid off his coolie, helped the trembling girl out of the vehicle and took her to the door.

The fat little sultan met him just inside the door. He said he was overwhelmed with delight at this honor his visitor was bestowing upon his humble hovel.

Sam said firmly: "Sultan, I appreciate this honor, but I

can't accept your daughter. She is a pearl beyond price, but there is no room for her in my life. And that's final!"

Turning, he walked out. The door closed, and the fat and perfumed little sultan, gazing at his youngest and loveliest daughter, said with scorn: "Well, little-arrow-that-speeds-true-to-its-mark?"

Koori smiled mysteriously. "When the red-headed man's schooner sails, I will sail also. Before I am through with that man, he will be on his knees to me."

12

SAMMY IS TRICKED

LOOKING FOR THE man who had crippled the Victory's engines might have been as hopeless an undertaking as looking for a needle in a haystack if it had not been for Singapore Sammy's personality. If, in looking for a needle in a haystack, you are equipped with a powerful electro-magnet, the needle is much less elusive.

With the coming of night, the city of Singapore had come noisily to life. The streets surged with men and women of every Far Eastern nationality. It was as if every house and every hovel had emptied its occupants into this hot and busy city which is truly the crossroads of the Orient.

If Bruno Reddy was anywhere in Singapore tonight, Singapore Sam believed he would find him. He had friends in countless quarters. He knew an ancient Hindu who trained cobras for street fakirs, and was an amazing source of current gossip. He knew a benign old Chinese who ruled the opium smuggling traffic in all Malaya—another prolific source of information. He knew a Jap, the head of a fishing company, who was, actually, the cleverest Japanese spy south of Hongkong. He knew beggars and thieves and dive-keepers. Many of them he had befriended at one time or another.

His first visit was to a Chinese undertaker's. The undertaker was an old and valued friend. From Chang Yin, Singapore Sam obtained no information, but he made all necessary arrangements for an elaborate Chinese funeral. He ordered a fine coffin, ornamented with gilt and red lacquer, and he ordered a score of professional mourners and priests, and a band. Leaving Chang Yin to carry out his directions, Singapore took a rickshaw to Jardine's godowns. From his friend Consadine at Jardine's, he purchased three 100-gallon water casks. He quested that the bands be loosened and one head of each be removed, and that the casks be placed on the wharf for delivery aboard the *Blue Goose* later.

His next call was to the residence of Ling Kee, which was a pebble's throw from Jardine's wharf. Ling Kee was a prosperous Chinese rice dealer. Singapore Sammy had once befriended him in Bangkok; had taken him and his son aboard the *Blue Goose* when an uprising against Chinese merchants had threatened the old rice dealer's life.

Ling Kee was somewhat horrified at the request Singapore made of him, but promised to coöperate.

With this final detail of his plans arranged, Sam now set forth on his hunt for Bruno Reddy.

He did not believe that the escaped oiler was the brains behind the vanishing of Ray Baxton, or the murder of Jeff Carmichael, or the killing last night of the man who wore the red sash, but he believed that Bruno Reddy could tell a great deal if he would talk. And Sam Shay, once he found the man, was sure he could make him talk freely.

He began making inquiries. It took him less than half an hour to establish the fact that Bruno Reddy was somewhere in Singapore. He naturally assumed that Bruno Reddy was in hiding, waiting for the chance to slip out of Singapore.

A Chinese parrot merchant on Rochore Road sent him to a blind beggar woman, stationed in front of the Hotel Europa. He saw her and gathered further information. The tenth person to whom Singapore went to for help was the sampan *fokie* who had taken Bruno Reddy to his hiding place the night before! Thus, in one hour, through friendship and the amazing grapevine telegraph of Singapore, did Sam Shay accomplish what the entire police force of the city had been vainly trying to accomplish for the past twenty-four.

In doing this, he unavoidably left a trail for the authorities to profit by—if they were fast enough. It was impossible, in the densely-thronged downtown streets, to shake off his trailers, and once they learned that he was on the prowl for the missing oiler, they would become doubly interested in Sam Shay's activities.

He did his best to shake off the pursuit when he learned about the sampan *fokie*. He took back alleys and doubled back here and there on his trail. And when he reached the waterfront, he was sure he was not followed.

Bruno Reddy was in hiding aboard the old City of Batavia, a packet freighter that had gone hard aground on Brani Reef in the August typhoon, and was at present abandoned, having been gutted by the harbor pirates while her owners quarreled over her in court.

She was about a mile from Sheer's Wharf, and almost

out of the water at low tide. A blinker buoy at either end of
her warned shipping of her presence. She carried no lights
of her own, but lay black and mysterious and sinister under
the blazing tropical stars.

THE THREE BULWARK gates, or ports, along her side, in
and out of which cargo had been trucked in the days of her
usefulness, hung open. As the sampan approached, Sam
could see through her betweendecks and out the square
hole on the other side.

The phosphorescence in the water was so green, so
bright, that it actually cast a glow against the square aper-
ture, and gave the illusion that black vapor was rising from
the port. In this amazing phosphorescent water, fish could
be seen clearly outlined. A harbor shark fully eight feet
long swam lazily along the barnacled hull at a depth of five
or six feet, with a stream of green fire playing like electric
sparks from the point of the dorsal and the flukes of the
powerful tail. The entire body of the fish was clearly visible
in its darkness against the surrounding green "water fire."

The sampan approached slowly, the *fokie* working the
sweep so deftly that no sound was made. Standing in the
bows, with his eyes fixed on the deck, Sam listened. He
heard nothing but the soft roaring of the city across Keppel
Harbor at his back, the soft gurgle of the incoming tide
about the stranded packet boat, and the scurrying of rats
aboard her.

Somewhere aboard that abandoned hulk a desperate
man was hiding. No doubt he was keeping a sharp lookout.
No doubt he was at this moment peering at the sampan
from one of the dozens of dark portholes along the side.
There were so many places for a man to hide aboard an

abandoned ship. And Singapore Sammy had had a suffi-
cient taste of Bruno Reddy's character. He was desperate
and dangerous—a wanted vandal and killer.

The sampan approached the rusted and barnacled bows.
The bow anchor was hanging cock-billed. It was festooned
with seaweed. The canted deck, which he could see as
the sampan moved silently along in the black water, was
littered with small wreckage not worth a harbor pirate's
trouble.

Running his eyes along the dark portholes, studying
the main deck for a sign of life, Singapore Sammy was
conscious of chills along his spine and a prickling at the
nape of his neck. It was risky business, going aboard this
old wreck. But it was necessary.

In Malay, Sam instructed the sampan boy to stand by
until summoned to wherever Sam blinked his pocket electric torch, three times.

Armed only with a pocket torch and the knife with
which, he was sure, the oiler had stabbed the man in the red
sash, Sam climbed up the anchor chain to the hawse-hole,
found precarious footing on the whalestreak and made his
way, inching, to the break of the deck well. The bulwarks
gate on the port side was out, too, and at this point he
stealthily made his entrance.

An army of rats scurried at the sound of his first cautious
footfall. He picked his way across the litter, aided only by
the reflected glow of Singapore against a cloud bank over
the business section, and by the fat silver stars which hung
brilliantly over the seaward side of the harbor. He would
not increase his disadvantage by using the pocket torch.

He passed the fo'c's'le door, which looked as if it had

been jammed. It was not a likely hiding place, nor were the paint or chain lockers. The likeliest place was the captains quarters, but Sammy did not go there at once. He took a devious course, going slowly, studying the shadows carefully before he advanced, fully aware of the risk he was running.

He proceeded along the orlop deck, and the only sounds of his progress were those made by scurrying rats. The old hulk was swarming with large and ravenous harbor rats. He reached the after end of the orlop without adventure, and cautiously climbed a steel ladder which went up to an opened manhole. Reaching the main deck, aft, he encircled the fantail house, peered in at the steering machinery, and cautiously started forward, pressing close against the superstructure wall until the after structure ended at the fiddley hatch, where he ventured out into the open again.

He took plenty of time. He only hoped that his quarry was unaware of his presence aboard. The captain's quarters were presumably on this deck, forward, on the starboard side, just under the wheelhouse.

It was darker on the starboard side of the ship, away from the glowing clouds above the city, and he advanced even more carefully than he had below. Guiding himself by the handrail, he reached the forward structure. He suddenly stopped, held his breath and listened. Over the pumping of his heart, accelerated by tension, he heard the now-familiar patter of rats' feet, and another sound. It was a scraping sound, as if a foot had scuffled.

HE WAITED, STARING straight ahead. The sky on the eastern horizon was so clear that he could see stars thickly sprinkled, and he was suddenly aware that a large object,

possibly a man, was being silhouetted against the random
sparklings of these stars. It was stationary. If the object in
silhouette was a man, the man was waiting for his next
move.

Testing this suspicion, Sam moved inboard from the rail,
but the riddle was not answered. Some large man-shaped
object still bulked motionless against the stars.

But as Singapore Sammy moved quickly to the left, the
object seemed to move also.

Without consciously willing it, Sam sprang toward the
suspicious object. His outstretched hands encountered a
thick mass of rope dangling from a davit. He seized it to
check his forward lunge. And instantly was attacked from
above!

A heavy load of fists and kicking legs dropped on him
from the roof of the forward structure. He did not have
time to twist or turn before he was carried to the deck on
hands and knees. His unseen assailant, profiting by that
surprise attack, was striking him about the unprotected
head and neck with fists or a club.

Sam, with a violent effort, got up, and the man hung
on his back, and wrapped his legs about Sam's middle,
and continued to send smashing blows into his head and
the back and sides of his neck. He tried to throw him off,
but the man clung. Ducking his head about in an attempt
to dodge those deadening blows, Sam braced himself a
moment, then ran backward toward the cabin wall.

The man on his back fetched up against a window, which
collapsed with a crunching of glass, and released his hold.
His breath must have been partially knocked out of him by
that surprise maneuver. He slid down, and Sam promptly

threw himself on him, striking out with both fists, some-times hitting flesh, sometimes the wood of the deck or the steel of the cabin wall.

The unseen man panted and gasped, and returned with ferocity to the attack. Sam fought with what was ebbing strength. He wanted only a handhold on his enemy, some point at which to apply the science of ju-jutsu. But his assailant was available only in the form of flailing fists and kicking feet.

Both men went down again, slugging and kicking and clawing, and fighting thus, rolled down the canted deck into the scuppers. A fist caught Sam fairly in the left cheek, and he clutched a handful of fingers, but they were wrenched from his grasp before he could bring pressure.

His next hold was a short and powerful neck. It was all muscle, and it was slimy with sweat. Again, he lost the chance. His hooked fingers slipped off, and a swinging boot found his shin.

The pain of that almost put him out of the fight, but he fought down the pain and resumed his drive for a hand-hold. He caught fingers again, but lost them. He found the neck again, and was driven off by blows in the face. His nose was bleeding. One eye would certainly be black.

He made another lunge and locked his fingers about a thick and hairy wrist. His other hand ran up a muscled arm, and, once again, found the neck. He took another punch in the left cheek to clinch his grasp on the neck. He found the nerve he was looking for and jammed down hard with his thumb.

It worked as effectively as an anesthetic. His powerful and savage assailant went as limp as sudden death.

13

REDDY TALKS

SINGAPORE SAMMY DID not want a corpse under his thumb. He wanted Bruno Reddy to deliver a long and useful monologue. Keeping the thumb in position, he reached out with the other hand and found a wrist. He rolled the half-conscious victim of Japanese wrestling science onto his face, forced the arm up behind his back, and felt for and found another sensitive spot.

When he withdrew his thumb from the man's neck, his prisoner uttered a deep and gasping groan.

"If you make a false move," the red-headed man panted, "I'll break this arm at the shoulder. Take it easy—and start talking."

"Who the hell are you?"

"Just a guy."

"That red-headed guy they call Singapore Sam?"

"You're right, Mr. Reddy. Now, talk."

"Sure, I'll talk. What the hell else can I do?"

"Who killed the wireless man on that yacht?"

"You mean Jeff Carmichael?"

"Yeah."

"Why are you so interested?"

"Don't get tough or I'll break this arm—and your neck, too. Stop stalling, Reddy. Talk."

"I'll talk, but I want to find out how you stand. Why do you suppose I'm in this—for my health?"

"You tell me, Mr. Reddy, and get to the point."

"Ouch! All right, all right! But why can't we pull it off together? There's more dough in it than you ever saw in your life!"

"Who from?"

"Ben Rosen. I could hang him! He gets a million a year from the Baxton Corporation. What I've got on him is worth two million. I'll split it with you. Ouch!"

"Quit stalling, smart guy, or it'll hurt."

"It ain't a stall! I'm tellin' yuh! It's Ben Rosen! He killed your pal and he killed Ray Baxton!"

"Yeah? Let's have the whole story. Let's hear why you crippled the port engine on the night of April sixth, and why you crippled the starboard engine on the way in yesterday?"

"Okay! Because I saw Ben Rosen stick a knife into Ray Baxton and throw him overboard! And I saw Ben Rosen stick a knife into your pal Jeff Carmichael and throw him overboard. I did it to attract attention. I figured the whole ship would turn out and they'd find Baxton and Jeff Carmichael missin'. But it didn't work."

"Why didn't you report it to your skipper?"

"Because I didn't want a knife in my back! How did I know who all was in on the deal?"

"The skipper?"

"Why not? It's bigger dough than any of 'em ever saw in their lives, ain't it?"

"How about that launch?"

"That launch snapped her towrope in the squall. That launch had nothin' to do with it."

"Why did Ben Rosen stab Jeff Carmichael?"

"Because Jeff saw him kill Baxton. Ben Rosen threw Baxton over the after rail. I just come above for a breath of fresh air before turnin' in. I saw Jeff come out of the after cabin just as Rosen threw Baxton over the rail. I saw Rosen follow Jeff up to the radio room and go in there and stick the knife into his back. I hid behind a lifeboat and saw him come out and throw Jeff overboard. Listen, Singapore Sam. I'm shootin' straight with you. I want you in on this. I gotta have help. It's too much for one man. It's a chance for the clean-up of a lifetime. Let me up, willya?"

"Not yet."

"But I want to show it all to you."

"What?"

"The write-up of it all. It's what I've been doin' ever since I've been hidin' out here—writin' it all up. I've got every detail of it. I've got names and dates and times. There's nothin' missin'. If you'll let me up, I'll show you. I've been workin' in the chief's room, between decks, tryin' to get it finished. It's almost finished. When it's finished I'm gonna put it in a safe deposit box in a bank, and I'm gonna let Ben Rosen know it's hid. If he tries anything fast—"

"Who was that guy in the red sash you killed?"

"It's all down in black on white. He was workin' with Rosen, but he split with Rosen, and he was tryin' to chisel in on me—blackmail. I rubbed him out because he was a chiseler. Take me down to the chief's cabin. I'm comin' clean, ain't I? Hold onto me any way you want, but take me down there, and if I'm lyin', you can twist my neck off. I've get everything in that write-up. I've got conversations and all the details. I've got a hundred pages written up. Take me to the chief's room and see for yourself."

Sam said: "Okay, Mr. Reddy. If you're lying, you'll regret it."

MAINTAINING HIS HOLD firmly on the captive wrist, Sam let his prisoner up. "If you try to kick, or break loose," he warned him, "I'll give this a twist."

"I'm no fool," the oiler said, and started aft.

Sam held onto the wrist firmly. Bruno Reddy led the way to a stairway aft. Sam held him with one hand and used his pocket torch with the other. Rats fled in waves from the white beam and from their approach. They went down the stairs and started along the orlop deck.

"It's half way forward, on the port side," the prisoner said.

Singapore Sammy had so far believed very little of what Bruno Reddy had told him. The oiler was bluffing. He knew it. Sam was taking him below decks, to the chief's room, simply to call that bluff. Once the bluff was called, Sam intended to bring a little more pressure to bear on Bruno Reddy's shoulder joint. He would learn the truth if it took all night.

Now and then, Sam turned the beam of the light into the oiler's face. It was done deliberately, to dazzle the man's eyes so that, if he suddenly played a trick, his eyes would be so blinded by the repeated glaring light that he would be at a serious disadvantage. And this trick was destined to have unforeseen results.

The oiler played his trick just as they were passing one of

the opened cargo ports. What his dazzled eyes did not see was the darkened harbor patrol boat that was approaching. He pretended to stumble. He cried: "Look out, I'm falling!"

And Sam momentarily released his hold. It was all Bruno Reddy needed. He snatched his wrist away, and he sprang toward the port.

As he did so, Sam saw the bow of the long and powerful police boat come slicing through the black water alongside.

He yelled: "Look out for that boat!"

The oiler turned his head as he ran. Sam caught only a twisted grin of scorn on the battered and bloody face of the oiler as he dived.

Sam ran to the port and looked down. He saw the sudden phosphorescence of the man's body added to the electric-green wake of the speeding boat. He could follow, as if in an animated X-ray, the passage of the escaping man under the hull—and his swift and horrible encounter with the propeller.

What had been the phosphorescent outline of a man became in an instant a shapeless whirling mass, which spun about in a blur and was then ejected.

Shivering, Sam flashed on his light. In the bright beam of it, the broken and mangled body came rolling to the surface, and Sam caught a dreadful glimpse of a head cleaved open from forehead to chin. Then the broken mass rolled over slowly and senselessly in the wake, and slowly sank.

The patrol boat had stopped. A man shouted an order. The softly humming engines were in reverse. A searchlight flashed on just as Singapore stepped back out of sight. He ran across the canted deck to the open port on the other

side, and blinked his pocket torch at the waiting *fokie* as a
signal to come alongside and take him off. In the time it
took the sampan boy to execute this order, Sam ran to the
chief's room and briefly investigated.

He was not disappointed to find no pile of manuscript.
He had known that Bruno Reddy was lying, perhaps in
all particulars, perhaps only in some. Yet what the oiler
had told him was ample proof that he had known the full
truth and could have given Sam valuable information if
he had desired. With his sudden and horrible death, Sam
realized, had gone his only hope of solving the murder of
Jeff Carmichael in Singapore.

As he was boarding the sampan, he was wondering just
what part Ben Rosen had played in that murder. He was
very anxious to meet the famous corporation lawyer.

The sampan was half way to shore when the patrol boat
overhauled it. The searchlight came on, picked out the
red-headed young man standing in the bows, and flooded
him with light. A voice shouted: "Sampan ahoy!"

"Ahoy, patrol boat!"

"Is that you, Captain Shay?"

"Aye!"

Silence ensued aboard the patrol boat, then the searchlight went dark. The patrol boat's engines gave a sullen
snort, and she shot ahead and vanished. It was evident that
all the police of Singapore had been ordered not to molest
Captain Shay tonight!

14

TOUGH CUSTOMER

SINGAPORE SAMMY LANDED on Pulau Hantu Point because it was farthest from the congestion of Singapore and nearest to his next objective, which was the Westover Rubber Plantation, four miles out on the Alexanura Road. He was now about to engage in the desperate undertaking of moving Ben Rosen, Dr. Hobb and Marthana Bondy from their hiding place to his schooner, the *Blue Goose*—without the knowledge of the newspaper men or the police!

Just how desperate an undertaking it might prove to be was indicated when he attempted to start out for the plantation in secrecy. He took a gharry. The gharry had not gone three city blocks before he discovered that he was being stalked by two men in rickshaws and one man afoot.

Reaching the Botanical Gardens, he resorted to a simple trick to shake off this pursuit. He reached up and slid a bill into his *syce's* hand and told him to keep driving. The gharry was approaching a deep shadow cast by a thicket beside the road. When the gharry reached the shadow, Singapore Sammy slipped out quietly and entered the thicket.

He crouched down in bushes, saw the two rickshaws pass, then the man afoot, and another gharry. He doubled back to a higher road, hailed another gharry, got into it and gave the *syce* directions.

The trick worked perfectly. Throughout the long drive to the Section Ten bungalow, he was not followed.

The Section Ten bungalow was on a private road of its own, a half mile from Alexanura Road and in the heart of the Section Ten rubber grove. Sam smelled the little settlement long before it appeared dimly in the starlight at a turn in the road. The familiar odors of hydrochloric acid, used in coagulating the latex, and the smell of smoldering wood from the curing sheds hung heavily in the hot, breathless night.

The bungalow was apparently bustling with activity. Lights blazed at all windows, and in the dooryard a large and picturesque assortment of Chinese had gathered. Near the porch lay a large and handsome Chinese coffin, but it was a coffin only in shape. Its coloring had been borrowed from a circus wagon. It was of bright red lacquer, with gilt and sky-blue ornaments. A Cantonese boy was squatted near it dolefully playing a three-stringed Chinese lute. In the darkness, a quartette mournfully sang.

All of this was in response to Singapore Sammy's orders, left with Chang Yin, the undertaker, some hours previously for a Chinese funeral befitting a mandarin.

Chang Yin walked out of the shadows from whence came the mournful tones of the quartette. Everything, he said to Sam in Malay, was in readiness. Where was the corpse?

Sam answered: "Where are the costumes?"

"In the coffin, *tuan.*"

A guttural voice projected itself from the doorway of the

bungalow. It irritably wanted to know what in the devil all this was about. Sam walked up onto the veranda. The man in the doorway was blond, fat and unmistakably Dutch. He stared at Singapore's red hair in the streaming light and cried: *"Ach Gott, mynheer!* You are Captain Shay, at last!"

"Yes."

"I am Torvin Van Vleet. You are welcome to my house. My guests are very nervous and impatient. Follow me, please!"

Sam followed him through large hot rooms and into a screened veranda at the rear of the house. A dim light burned on a table and showed Sam the pale, drawn faces of three people—two men and a slim blond girl.

All three were standing, facing the doorway. They stared at him as he strode in, and Marthana Bondy cried: "Oh, Sam, Sam! I'm so glad you're here!" In her white linen dress, she looked younger than she had last night. But her face looked older. It was wan with fatigue.

The two men had not moved. Both looked haggard. He recognized them at once as the mysterious pair he had seen last night in the beef wood thicket—the elderly hunchback, Ben Rosen, and the late Oliver Baxton's personal physician, Dr. Elton Hobb.

The famous corporation lawyer was chewing an unlighted cigar. Dr. Hobb stood with folded arms and regarded Singapore Sammy with an air of fatigued amusement.

BEN ROSEN SAID in a heavy, throaty voice: "So you're Captain Shay!"

"The famous Captain Shay!" Dr. Hobb added in an amused voice.

The girl said quickly: "What's happened?"

"Just a moment," the lawyer drawled, shifting his cigar to the other corner of his mouth. He placed his hands on his hips and stared steadily at the red-headed man in the doorway. He said again, "So you're Captain Shay!"

Sam had not been prepared for hostility. He said quietly, "Is there any question about it?"

"I want to have a talk with you," the lawyer said, in that heavy, throaty voice.

"There isn't much time for talking," Sam answered. "Every policeman and secret service man in Singapore is looking for you. If you want to get aboard my schooner, there's no time to waste."

"Just—one—moment," Ben Rosen said slowly. "I want to know what's been done and what's being done. I would like some kind of report."

"Won't that wait?" Sam said mildly.

"It will not!"

Marthana groaned: "Oh, Lord! Can't you forget for a minute that you're not addressing a board meeting? Captain Shay is an expert. We've placed our troubles in his hands. We're taking his orders."

Ben Rosen said harshly: "Before another step is taken, I insist on knowing what has happened and what this fellow's plans are!"

"But you heard him say there isn't time!"

The hunchback ignored her. "You can make your report now, captain. What have you found out?"

Sam quietly answered, "Nothing of importance, We have to go to the island."

"Did you find Bruno Reddy?"

"I did. I tracked him to a derelict in the harbor where he had holed up. He got away from me, jumped overboard and got fouled in the screw of a police boat."

The hunchback stared intently at Sam's green eyes. Ben Rosen's eyes were brown and velvety, and Sam wondered if his brusqueness, his air of importance, his suspicious attitude were a deliberate pose. He knew how shrewd, how clever and how ruthless this man must be. He was a deep one. If he was playing a game, it would be a clever one. A man brilliant enough to earn a million a year from an American corporation didn't deal in simple schemes.

"How about that fellow in the red sash?"

"I found him at the door of my hotel bedroom with a knife in his back."

"When?"

"Dawn."

"Dead?"

"Yes."

"Who did it?"

"Bruno Reddy."

The velvety eyes were narrow and watchful. "What else have you done, Captain Shay?"

"Made all the necessary arrangements to get you aboard my schooner, as Miss Bondy requested."

"Secretly?"

"That's right."

"Very well," Ben Rosen said, in that heavy, throaty voice; "before we proceed to a consideration of your plan—"

"There's no time to discuss anything more," Sam said impatiently.

"Look out for that boat!" Sam yelled.

"No," Marthana firmly agreed. "There'll be time to talk on the schooner. Sam, are these Chinese—"

"I insist," the hunchback broke in, "on a distinct understanding before we take another step." His contemptuous attitude was more and more irritating.

Marthana said: "Now look here, Mr. Rosen; Captain Shay knows this part of the country. He's not a hireling. I know you're upset. We're all upset. But I insist—"

"I was coming to that," the hunchback stopped her again. "Just how much is this worth to you, Captain Shay—what you've done since Marthana contacted you, and the use of your services and schooner for this undertaking?"

SAM DID NOT answer. His Irish was up. He knew that Ben Rosen was upset, and he suspected that Ben Rosen was accustomed to authority and power. In this predicament he was powerless, and it doubtless angered him to have to rely on someone else.

Marthana said swiftly: "I think you're taking the wrong approach. Sam isn't a hireling. He's in this entirely because his best friend was murdered."

"Thank you, Marthana," the hunchback said coldly. "I happen to have had a certain amount of experience with men and with money. What's your price, Captain Shay?"

"Miss Bondy is right," Sam said, controlling himself. "I'm not in this for the money."

The shrewd eyes hardened. "Captain Shay, if you think for a moment that, just because you're working for the Baxton Corporation, you're going to hold us up—"

"I don't give a damn about—" Sam began hotly.

Marthana cried: "Mr. Rosen!"

"Who is this fellow?" the hunchback shouted. "What do I know about him? What are his credentials?"

"He's a friend of Jeff Carmichael's!" Marthana said angrily. "That's enough for me."

"Aren't you apt to be a little biased?" Dr. Hobb asked. The tall, handsome young man had been standing some distance apart, with his hands in his pants pockets, his expression one of whimsical amusement. "It seems to me," he drawled, "that Mr. Rosen is right in making all these arrangements beforehand."

"But I tell you," the girl cried, "Sam isn't interested in money. I begged him to help us, and he's willing, but only because of Jeff!"

"And I won't take a step," the hunchback snarled, "until we know exactly where we stand and what this fellow's plans are. This is a dangerous and delicate situation. No one must suspect that Ray Baxton did not come ashore here;

no one must suspect that we have slipped out of Singapore. There must be no bungling."

"Like the smallpox case?" Sam asked. He had been trying to control himself, but Ben Rosen's bullying methods and Dr. Hobb's air of smiling contempt were too much for him. "Every man aboard the yacht was suspicious. And how do I know what was really back of it? What are your credentials?"

The hunchback and the doctor made a sudden movement toward him as if they were going to attack him. Whatever the impulse was, they checked it. And whether it was merely a betrayal of nerves at the cracking point, or the involuntary confession of two rogues at whom suspicion was unexpectedly pointed Sam could not say.

Ben Rosen said harshly: "How we chose to handle our problem before you were called in is none of your business. I have asked you two pointblank questions. I want answers to both. What are your plans for getting us secretly out of Singapore, and how much do you want for your services and your charter?"

"We're going through Singapore as part of a funeral procession," Sam answered quietly, "and I'm going to charge the Baxton Corporation just what it costs, and not a dollar more."

"Let's go," Marthana said.

"Not yet!" the hunchback barked. "I'm not through with this fellow yet. I'm not satisfied—"

"There's no more time for squabbling," Sam said grimly. "There'll be a week or ten days for it on the schooner. Do you want to go aboard, or do you want to stay here? Make up your mind!"

"I won't be talked to—"

"Okay. Suit yourself. I'm not wasting any more time. I'm going to Murder Island. You can go or not as you damned please. Marthana!"

"There's no argument," she said crisply. "I've got utter and complete faith in you, and I'm sick and tired of people who can't take simple orders given by an expert."

Sam glanced at the hunchback, then at the doctor. "How about you two? Make up your minds! Are you coming or aren't you?"

Ben Rosen was glaring at him. "Yes."

"Yes," Dr. Hobb said.

15

CHINESE FUNERAL

SAM RAISED HIS voice and called Torvin Van Vleet.
He came in, pale and anxious-looking. Sam said to him,
in Malay: "Tell Chang Yin to bring that coffin in here."
And when the Dutchman had departed on this errand:
"Where's your luggage?"

"In here." Marthana opened a door which gave upon a
large closet and disclosed a small mountain of suitcases.
"Can you handle it all?"

"Yep. Before I tell you about this plan, there's another
important point to be settled. This whole colony is in an
uproar over Ray's Baxton's disappearance. Are you going
to leave that up in the air?"

Marthana answered: "That's what we were arguing about
when you came in. It's what we've been arguing about all
day long. Have you a suggestion?"

Torvin Van Vleet returned, still looking anxious.

"Yes," Sam said. "You have gone on a month's tiger hunt
with the Maharaja of Johor. He lives just across the straits.
He is an old friend of mine and will back me up. You and
Ray Baxton, hating all this publicity, have gone to Johor
and are now guests of the maharaja. *Mynheer* Van Vleet,
how does that strike you?"

The Dutchman nodded vigorously. "It is perfect."

"Give us a chance to get through town—about two hours—then telephone all the newspapers, the consulates and the governor's residence. Mr. Baxton and these people did not wish their whereabouts to be known until they were safely away."

"Very good, *mynheer*," the Dutchman affirmed.

"You can say something to the effect that Mr. Baxton is disgusted with all this curiosity; that he is grieving over his father's death, and wanted absolute privacy." Sam looked at Ben Rosen. "Is that satisfactory?"

The lawyer worked his lips. His eyes remained hostile. It was evident that any order not given by himself went very much against the grain.

"Yes!" Marthana cried. "It's a marvelous idea, Sam. Now—about the funeral."

"We're having what is known as a Tai Pan's funeral. That means a Number One funeral, such as is given a mandarin, and will attract more attention but cause less curiosity than an ordinary funeral." He didn't explain that paradox, but went on: "I'm sure I wasn't tracked here. Chang Yin is absolutely trustworthy. We have only to play our parts. I'll explain that in a moment."

Chang Yin and his oldest son had come in with the coffin. The two Chinese removed the lid. The coffin contained blue and white garments. "These," Sam explained, "are our disguises. In these pots are make-up. Chang Yin, being a clever undertaker, is clever at the art of make-up. We are to be made up as Chinese, of course. We are mourners."

"What do we do?" Ben Rosen grumbled.

"You mourn."

The highest salaried corporation lawyer in the United States made no further protest, although he grumbled and muttered to himself. While Chang Yin busied himself making the faces of Ben Rosen, Marthana Bondy and Dr. Hobb resemble, as closely as the art of make-up would permit, the faces of Orientals, Sam and Chang Yin's son packed the luggage into the coffin. There was room enough for it all.

And while Sam was making up his own face at a mirror and adjusting a black wig over his fiery red hair, Chang Yin and his son were carrying the coffin outside and forming the procession.

Marthana went to another room to change into her costume. All the garments were the blue and white of Chinese mourning. When Sam had changed, the lawyer and the doctor were ready, and when Marthana returned, wearing a black wig, a long, white jacket buttoned to her neck, and loose blue trousers, he looked the three of them over critically. They might not have passed close scrutiny in the daylight, but they were passable enough for a night inspection.

And of them all, Ben Rosen could most easily have fooled the sharpest eyes. It was amazing to Sam that the hunchback, with his prominent Semitic features, should have become, with the aid of a little greasepaint, so perfectly Chinese. In his white and blue garments, with the little black cap on his head, he might have been an elderly and benevolent mandarin.

WHEN THEY WENT outside, the procession was formed and ready to start. Torch bearers led the way. They were followed by the cymbal-beaters. The purpose of these was to drive devils from the path and vicinity of the coffin.

Behind the cymbal-beaters were Buddhist priests, in funereal white, each swinging a smoking incense pot. Their purpose was to prepare the way for the departing spirit into the first of the several layers, or heavens, of Nirvana, the ultimate heaven. Behind the priests came the mourners, the four disguised Americans and a score of hired mourners who would wail and beat their chests with their fists in despair.

The coffin followed the mourners. Behind it was the band, numbering fourteen pieces, which would play continuously. The rear was brought up by the banner-bearers, a dozen in all. White banners, carried on tall staffs, set forth the merits of the departed. Chang Yin carried these in stock—sentiments to suit the merits of anyone, from a poet to a merchant prince. And scattered along the procession were the dragon boys. The dragons were of paper, and of different bright colors. They floated and rippled at the end of sticks, as the boys ran in and out of the procession.

The purpose of the dragons was a dubious one, which Sam Shay had never quite understood. They had to do with immortality, or with the hopes of the deceased for a re-birth in a better world. Like the word "maskee," the dragon could mean almost anything. It was a symbol of royalty, it was an emblem of the highest courage, and it stood for death and a hundred things in between.

Sam and his protégés took their places among the hired mourners and the procession got under way. It could, of course, be heard for miles. This plan, if it worked, was a sound one, and was based on the old rule; to avoid attention, attract as much as possible.

As they fell in with the hired mourners, Sam explained to his companions: "The best way to attract attention is to do nothing. Mourners howl, sob, yell, beat their breasts, and tear their hair. Be careful of your wigs!"

Dr. Hobb might have been a youthful Chinese business man. Marthana, in the light of the torches, was a demure and lovely Chinese maiden. She fell into her part promptly, and convincingly. She sobbed. She beat her breast, as the other women mourners were doing.

The doctor showed almost as much willingness and adeptness. At first, he was self-conscious, but it was not hard to fall into the spirit of the occasion, with the hired mourners playing their parts so well. Soon he, too, was howling and beating his chest.

Ben Rosen was the slowest of them all. His fierce resentment at being ordered about still showed itself, but when Sam said to him, almost savagely: "Get busy and mourn!" the hunchback began howling, too. Then he, too, fell into the spirit of it.

As Chinese funerals are always noisy, and as such processions, because of the large Chinese population, are everyday occurrences in Singapore at all hours of the day and night, in spite of the efforts of the British to confine them to the daylight hours, Sam Shay's "Tai Pan funeral" entered the city without attracting more than casual notice.

Vehicles drew off the road. Most of the spectators, aside from tourists, who gave the procession more than passing notice, were other Chinese, whose interest was not in the mourners but in the size of the procession and the elegance of the coffin. Some of them followed the procession.

It took Sam's funeral two hours, marching in the straightest possible line, to reach the mansion of his old friend Ling Kee, the rice dealer.

Ling Kee, fat and perspiring, and more than a little frightened because of the blasphemy of it, welcomed the funeral to his compound. The cymbal-beaters surrounded him at the doorway, so that evil spirits would not enter the house. The coffin was carried inside. Four of the mourners accompanied it into Ling Kee's ceremonial parlor. The others remained in the compound, the band still playing, the mourners still howling and beating their chests, the banner-bearers moving slowly about so that the curious could read the sentiments emblazoned on the white flags, and the dragon boys running about the compound and shouting.

The four mourners who had accompanied the coffin into Ling Kee's ceremonial parlor were, of course, Singapore Sammy and his three protégés. He was reasonably sure that his scheme was successful so far. Throughout the course of the procession, he had watched the sidewalk crowds; had seen colonial spies among them, and was sure that his elaborate scheme for spiriting the lawyer, the doctor and the girl out of Singapore was so far unsuspected. The next step was, however, more precarious.

Under cover of the darkness—and the bedlam in the compound—he must smuggle all the luggage and his three protégés into Jardine's nearest godown, which adjoined Ling Kee's back yard.

The coffin would remain in this parlor for a day and

be appropriately mourned over by the priests and hired
mourners, then the band, the priests, the mourners, the
banner-bearers and the dragon boys would be dismissed,
and the coffin would be smuggled back to Chang Yin's
undertaking parlors.

THE LUGGAGE WAS removed from the coffin and carried
by coolies into the godown. Ling Kee engaged the Chinese
watchman at Jardine's in conversation outside the godown
while Sammy helped Ben Rosen, Dr. Hobb and Marthana
into the 100-gallon casks, piled luggage about them, fitted
the three lids in place, and tightened the hoops.

In the darkness of Ling Kee's backyard, he removed
the wig and stripped off his mourning garments. These he
used to scrub the make-up from his face. He had worn his
jacket and white ducks under the mourning garments, so
that he was once again the man the Singapore police, the
Singapore newspapermen and the colonial spies were so
anxious to find.

He returned to the godown, briskly told the watchman
to have the three casks put aboard the *Blue Goose* immediately, and returned once more to the busy congestion of the
Singapore streets. He was promptly found by the vigilant
secret service and trailed all the way back to the *Blue Goose!*

The red-headed man was a little alarmed when he saw
the congestion on Sheer's Wharf and aboard the schooner. Newspapermen and cameramen were lounging about.
Representatives of the governor and of the American
consul were waiting for him.

A small roar went up when he appeared, and he was
promptly surrounded. The fact that the yacht Victory had
entered the harbor of Singapore without the Baxton crown

prince aboard was now apparently established to everyone's satisfaction. And it was equally certain that the red-headed and mysterious schooner captain not only knew much more than he cared to admit, but was the only man in Singapore who knew anything at all about it! The complete disappearance of Ben Rosen, Dr. Hobb and Marthana Bondy had made the mystery more tantalizing than ever. Where were they? What was it all about?

On his way to the end of the dock, Sam was asked by upward of a score of men where they were.

"I don't know."

"Where's Ray Baxton?"

"Gentlemen, I don't know."

"Are you clearing?"

"I am. Chop-chop!"

This news went through the gathering in another small roar. The Eurasian secret service man who had spoken so sternly to Sam outside the jail grabbed him by the elbow. He looked ugly.

"Where are you going, captain?"

"Aboard my ship. I've got a clearance for San Francisco. If you don't believe it, ask the harbor master. Ask the American consul!"

He shook off the Eurasian's hand and went aboard. Flashlights flashed.

The *Blue Goose* was swarming with men. Rufe Pound met him at the rail. He looked haggard and bewildered.

"Skipper," he panted, "what the hell is it all about? I tried to keep 'em off. They've been through this ship from stem to stern the past three hours like a swarm o' rats. What's up?"

"We're checking out as soon as Jardine's boat puts some new water casks aboard. Have they come?"

"Not yet. What—"

"We're clearing the minute they come. Stow them in Number One hold."

MEN CAME FILING out of the companionway as Sam went aboard. They looked serious. The opinion seemed to prevail that Sam Shay was up to some of the trickery for which he was so notorious. His only fear was that his permission to clear might be countermanded at the last moment. He was the key to Singapore's latest and most baffling mystery.

More reporters and secret service men surrounded him on the after deck.

"Where is Ben Rosen?"

"I don't know."

"I'll bet you don't know!"

"You're right, mister!"

He saw Jardine's supply launch approaching. It came alongside. Chills raced along his spine when he saw the three large new casks, as yellow as butter, each suddenly as large and conspicuous as a burning hotel.

It seemed incredible that those three casks would come aboard unsuspected. Rufe Pound was bawling orders. He was forward, near the hatch into which the casks would be lowered.

More grim-looking men filed up from below. Most of them wore white drill. The knees of many looked as if they had been crawling about on them, and Sam realized that these men, reporters and secret service men, had had orders to search the ship minutely.

He was fascinated by the three large casks, but he forced

himself not to look in that direction. He wanted no more
attention than necessary attracted to those three precious
casks.

An order was shouted. Blocks creaked. Sam said generally to the tense, hard-faced men surrounding him: "Well,
gentlemen, are you satisfied that I'm telling you the truth?"

"Certainly not!" a stout, red-faced man snapped. "You're
up to some of your tricks. You're going to try to smuggle
those three people out of Singapore!"

Sam looked at him with cold green eyes. "Why should
I?"

"I don't know," the red-faced man sputtered. "Why are
you always up to some mischief?"

"I'll tell you the truth," Sam said. "I'm sick of all this.
That's why I'm checking out. Since last night, I've been
thrown in jail twice. I've been hounded and persecuted. I
want to get away from it all." He saw the second cask come
swinging aboard and drop slowly into the forward hatch.
He shouted: "All visitors ashore, please!"

There was a reluctant movement toward the dock.
Perhaps twenty-five pairs of eyes were watching him. He
had never seen so much concentrated suspicion in his life.

A winch engine clattered and hissed. An empty hook
on the end of a line soared out of the forward hatch. One
more cask!

"All visitors ashore, please!" Sam herded them toward
the rail. "Unless you gentlemen want a ride to San Francisco, you'd better get off this ship!"

A coolie aboard the Jardine supply boat was throwing
a loop about the last cask. Men began climbing from the
Blue Goose to the dock. A voice yelled an order and the

third cask sailed up into the air. Out of the tail of his eye, Sam watched it—and, to his horror, it continued to sail!

The third cask had slipped from the loop. It struck the rail of the schooner a glancing blow and caromed off into the water.

16

STOWAWAY

RUFE POUND WAS roaring curses in pidgin at the careless coolie on the supply boat. Someone caught the rim of the cask with a boathook. Hands pulled it aboard the supply boat.

The stout-faced man said suspiciously: "What's in those casks?"

Singapore Sammy gave every evidence of a man robbed of the last shred of his patience. His eyes blazed. He clenched his big fists.

"I'll tell you!" he roared. "It's Ray Baxton! He's chopped up in fine pieces! Get the hell off this ship! Willie! Throw off those lines! Rufe! Get that cask stowed aboard and start the engine!"

He must have given a convincing display of temper. He wondered who was in that third cask, and hoped it wasn't Marthana. He heard the thud of it as it struck the deck at the bottom of the hold. Rufe disengaged the tackle and ran aft. The *serang* was casting off the lines. The deck under Sam's heels throbbed as the auxiliary engine came to life.

The last of Sam's visitors climbed over the rail and jumped to the dock as the *Blue Goose* began to move. Sam, at the wheel, looked along the line of white, brown and red faces. More questions were shouted at him. He answered none of them. Clear of the dock, he put the wheel over and dubiously eyed the shipping which cluttered the roadstead. There were still so many chances for a slip-up! At the last moment, the governor might send a patrol boat after him and order him back for another inquiry.

The disabled Victory, as white as a moth, as deserted as a graveyard, fell astern. Sam wondered what kind of a day Captain Jayne had put in.

He caught himself holding his breath until the pulses in his ears thumped. A patrol boat crossed his wake a hundred yards astern. Her searchlight flashed on, centered on him, flashed off.

At five knots, the *Blue Goose* slipped through the roadstead and stood out to sea. The lights of shipping dimmed, and the glow of Singapore sank lower on the horizon. But the danger wasn't yet past. When Tanjong Teregeh was well astern, Sam called the mate and *serang* aft and instructed them to search the ship from cutwater to counter for stowaways.

The search took them an hour. When they reported that the ship had been thoroughly searched, he ordered the sails raised and the engine stopped. A good breeze from the northwest was springing up. Sam gave the wheel to Rufe and said: "The course is due south through the Karimata. Are you sure that girl isn't aboard?"

"That native cutie? No, skipper. I know she ain't aboard. She come aboard about an hour after you took her away the last time and I shooed her off. She come aboard again about an hour before we checked out, and I shooed her off again. She ain't aboard. No, sir. No stowaways!"

Sam went forward with a lantern, and descended into Number One hold. He called: "Marthana!"

Her voice, muffled, answered from one of the casks: "Hi!"

He loosened the loops, pried up the lid with his fingers and pulled it off. Marthana was crouched on the bottom, surrounded with bags and suitcases. Her Chinese make-up had melted and run. She was so stiff that Sam had to lift her out. Her legs were asleep. She was nearly fainting from the heat.

"Sorry I couldn't let you out sooner," Sam said. "I had to make sure there weren't any stowaways."

Muffled yells came from the other casks. Sam said: "Who bounced overboard?" And the muffled voice of the doctor answered: "I did!"

Sam freed the two men and helped them out. The lawyer was in a state of collapse, from the heat. Dr. Hobb, in spite of his fall, was unhurt.

When they were rested and had stretched their muscles, Sam took them above and aft. Rufe, at the wheel, stared at the procession as if he were seeing disembodied spirits.

"Stowaways?" he blurted.

"Passengers," Sam answered.

"Chinks!" Rufe growled. "What are we doin' with Chinks?"

"Americans," Sam answered. "You watch the wheel, Rufe, and don't strain that brain of yours."

He took the passengers below and to their cabins. All three wanted to bathe and change. Sam showed them the showers, then he called Ah Fat and told him to fetch their luggage.

He went on to his own room. He was suddenly dog-tired.

He had been on the go, without sleep, for more than thirty-six hours. He was hungry and dirty and disgruntled. He poured himself a stiff drink of Scotch and sat on the edge of his bunk to drink it.

He told himself that he wasn't clever. He was nothing but the hard-boiled skipper of a trading schooner, and he was going to match his wits against one of the smartest, cleverest lawyers in the United States—a man who was a master at the arts of deception, guile and intrigue. He had only one advantage: he knew these countries better than Ben Rosen did.

Sam tossed off the drink and decided to take a bath and change into fresh clothes. He went to his closet for a clean white suit. There were white jackets and white duck pants hanging in a neat row on hangers. Below, on the floor, were light-weight white shoes in a neat row. Above, on the shelf, were sun helmets of various sizes and shapes—six of them in a neat row.

As he reached into the closet to take down a coat, one of the sun helmets mysteriously bounded from the shelf, struck him on the head, bounced and flew halfway across the room.

Something moved. He caught the gleam of jade-green silk behind the row of sun helmets. This was puzzling, because nothing was kept behind the sun helmets but a pile of work pants. Then he caught a familiar intoxicating perfume. Next he saw a pair of shining dark eyes.

"Koori!" Sam cried.

17

WOMEN STICK TOGETHER

THE PRINCESS OF Saballa wriggled, giggled, rolled over, pushed the rest of the sun helmets off the shelf, and swung her legs over the edge. Sun helmets fell all about Sam and went bouncing to all parts of the cabin.

Koori clasped her small golden hands about her knees, grinned radiantly and burst into an explanation in Saballanese, with gestures. She waved her hands and kicked her feet.

"Come on down out of there!"

Sam held up his hands. She held out her arms, jumped, squealed, and imprisoned his head in her strong young arms. She kissed him and cuddled tight against him.

The red-headed man patiently pried her fingers from his neck; gripped her securely by the waist and tossed her none too gently to the bunk, on which she landed safely; bounced once and remained upright with the apparent permanence of a barnacle, and laughed joyously as if it were all a jolly lark.

He went to the doorway and yelled: "Rufe! Come here!"

Rufe yelled for the *serang* to relieve him at the wheel, and came below. He walked into the room, stopped, stared at Koori and said plaintively: "Well, can you feature that!"

"You shooed her off," Singapore reminded him.

"Sure, I shooed her off. Twice! How did she do it?"

"She doesn't speak English."

Rufe lost his look of chagrin. He said: "She don't have to, skipper. What you gonna do with her?" And when Sam did not answer: "I guess maybe it's the hand of fate, skipper. If I was you, I'd quit tryin' to lose her. My, but ain't she cute! Look at them eyes! Look at them cute little hands and feet! She's just like a doll, ain't she? Skipper!" he cried.

"Yeah?"

"Get a load of them lashes! They're an inch long! Just lookin' at them lashes—don't it make you feel affectionate all over?"

"No."

"Skipper, you sure must be made o' stone. Look at that shape. If that ain't the cutest shape—"

He stopped. The door had opened. Ah Fat came waddling in. He stared at Koori, then at Sam and said amiably: "My, my, my! What thing hab got?"

"Lemme answer that one," Rufe said. "The skipper's got him a gal, and he don't seem to know what to do with her."

"Mally the lady," Ah Fat said promptly. "Velly plitty. Velly cozy. Maskee!"

"I believe," Sam said suspiciously, "you two fatheads knew this girl was hiding in that closet. You smuggled her on board!"

His two loyal employees protested violently. Too violently, perhaps. Sam was convinced that Ah Fat, that sentimental Oriental, had been the ringleader. But when accused, the cook was so volubly wounded, so eloquently indignant, that Singapore had difficulty in restraining a grin. At any rate, the thing was done, and punishing the two protesting romantics would not help matters.

Singapore said sternly, "I've been trying to tell you that we've got a tough job on our hands. We're going to Murder Island. Before we get back, there's going to be blood spilled. You can chalk that up right now. We've got one woman aboard already. One's plenty. We can't put back to Singapore. We can't put in any place. We have got to dodge the steamers. What are we going to do with her—throw her overboard with a bunch of belaying pins tied around her neck?"

"Put in at Borneo," Rufe suggested. "There's plenty of deserted coastline on Borneo. But it would be a crime. It would be murder. Them savages would eat her alive!"

"Too much silly talkee," Ah Fat growled. "Why not mally the lady? Velly plitty. Make velly nice litty wife."

"No," Sam said firmly.

"How much wanchee?" Ah Fat replied briskly. "Mebby I mally."

Sam looked at him sternly. "Ah Fat, you're an unprincipled scoundrel."

"Ah Fat's right," Rufe declared. "Just look at her, skipper! What's the matter with her? Ain't she a little dream o' feminine beauty?"

The three men looked at Koori critically, as if for flaws. Her eyes sparkled like jewels. They darted from face to face, but they returned to Sam's. She smiled at him radiantly.

"She's pretty enough," Sam said. "But I don't want her."

"Why not?" Rufe demanded.

"I don't want a woman."

"Don't you like her?"

"I don't want her."

"Skipper, take a good look at her."

"I am looking at her."

"And you still don't want her?"

"No."

"Well," said the golden-skinned maiden on the bed, in perfectly clear English, "that ought to settle it. He doesn't want me."

THE THREE MEN stared at the lovely island princess, and Sam said, in a thick voice, "What's that?"

Koori got down from the bunk. She was not more than five feet tall, but she was as belligerent as a fleet of dreadnaughts.

"If you think I'm enjoying this," she said swiftly, "if you think it's a pleasure to sit here and be insulted by three hulking brutes—"

"Wait a minute," Singapore said. "Major Ram Singh said you didn't speak English. You brought it on yourself. Speaking for my crew, we apologize. Now, kindly explain yourself."

Her huge, dark eyes lingered on his mysteriously. She wasn't smiling now, and the absence of her smile gave her small, golden face another kind of beauty, mysterious and dazzling.

"My father has been trying to get rid of me for a year. He is practically penniless. When you saved his life, it was a heaven-sent opportunity. He thought you were a soft-hearted American."

Sam suspected that she was lying. "There's nothing I can do," he said, "but put you ashore at the nearest land. That's Borneo."

Koori's eyes were suddenly large with terror. "Oh, you can't do that! I've never been anywhere alone. I've never traveled alone!"

"Where," Rufe asked, "did you learn to speak English so good?"

"In a Hongkong convent school," she answered, without moving her large, frightened eyes from Sam's. "You won't put me ashore. Please don't put me ashore!"

Ah Fat had left the corridor door ajar. A face peeped in. Blue eyes grew wide with excitement, and Marthana caroled: "How perfectly delicious! Am I intruding?"

"No," Singapore said. His face was suddenly scarlet. "Come in, Miss Bondy."

Marthana was wearing a fresh white dress. She looked cool and crisp after her shower.

"A stowaway," Singapore explained. "She was hiding on the shelf in my closet."

The blond girl looked at Koori with a puzzled smile. The contrast between her golden-haired, white-skinned blondness and the island girl's golden coloring, with her blue-black hair and thick black lashes, was startling, but Sam wasn't aware of it.

"Mebby I talkee, huh?" Ah Fat inquired helpfully. "Last night, taipan, he go 'longside that alley. In that alley he look-see big bhobbery. That black man him tly snag li'l missy's papa's—"

"Somebody else had better try," Marthana interrupted. "I'm a stranger here myself."

"Ah Fat," Sam explained, "is trying to say that I was in a rickshaw last night when this young lady's father was being attacked by black footpads. I happened to scare them off and he was so grateful that he gave me a lot of presents, including—including her. She's just told me that her father is broke and has been trying for a year to get rid of her, and he figured that, being an American, I—"

"That," Marthana interrupted, "doesn't make it much fun for her."

Koori was looking at the blond girl hopefully. She said: "He wants to put me ashore. I'd be terrified. I've never traveled or been anywhere alone."

"You can share my room," Marthana said promptly. "It has two bunks."

"We can't take her along," Sam said firmly.

"What are you going to do with her, then? She can't swim back to Singapore, and we can't put back, and we can't put in at any port, can we?"

"No," Sam admitted. "But—" He stopped, because he couldn't say what he thought. Possibly Koori was telling the truth. Possibly that incident with the footpads and the Sultan of Saballa in the alley hadn't been a deliberate and clever trick. Possibly Koori's persistence was nothing but a docile observance of old Oriental customs.

At any rate, she had him coming and going. There was no possible way of getting rid of her. She would have to stay on the *Blue Goose.* But Singapore resolved to watch her.

"And now that's settled," Marthana said firmly.

"You wait," Ah Fat said. He nodded genially at Sam. "You like?"

The island princess said to Marthana, "Thank you. If you hadn't been here—" She did not finish, but glanced sorrowfully at Sam. "Borneo!" she murmured.

"Oh, he wouldn't have put you ashore on Borneo,"

Marthana said cheerfully. "He's terrible, but not that terrible. Come on."

MARTHANA TOOK THE Princess of Saballa to her cabin, and Sam's last recollection of Koori that night, as she left his room, was of her large, wistful eyes, her faint, mysterious smile. It was such a look as a woman in love might have given her lover, and it made Sam feel extremely uncomfortable.

Ben Rosen, when he heard of the stowaway, was cynical. And when Sam told him of the circumstances of the sultan's rescue, he was skeptical and suspicious. He was evidently determined to be quarrelsome and troublesome, to assert his authority, and to show Singapore Sammy that he had a very low opinion of him.

Their conference in the dining room did nothing to relieve the tension. Sam tried to conceal his growing suspicion of the hunchback and the doctor, and as for them, neither made any attempt at concealing his mysterious resentment of Sam.

As if Sam were a suspicious character on the witness stand, the lawyer questioned and cross-questioned him. He tried to trick Sam into contradictions. Sam, for his part, shot questions at Ben Rosen that were, if not confusing, at least infuriating.

He wanted to know just what Ben Rosen had seen on the after deck of the yacht on the night Ray Baxton disappeared. He wanted to know why Ben Rosen hadn't concocted some better scheme to hoodwink the crew than the smallpox hoax. He wanted to know why Ben Rosen hadn't, immediately on wakening from his drunken stupor, ordered the captain to put about and make a search for the young man.

To none of these questions could Ben Rosen give satisfactory answers. Sam and Marthana sat on one side of the table, and Ben Rosen and the doctor sat on the other, facing them. Thus were these forces aligned—Ben Rosen and Dr. Hobb *versus* Sam and Marthana. And thus they were aligned to the end.

When Ben Rosen accused Marthana of suspecting him of complicity in the disappearance of Ray Baxton, she said: "You're too smart for an inexperienced girl. I don't know."

Ben Rosen glared at her, but carried the discussion no further. He was very nervous. He drummed on the table, he stroked his nose, he chewed one cold cigar after another. Watching him, Sam's suspicions continued to grow.

Dr. Hobb said little, only a word now and then to defend or affirm the hunchback. His attitude was one of amusement. When Sam spoke, the handsome young doctor watched him with an air of scorn or contempt.

A golden dawn was at the portholes when Marthana jumped up and said that all this bickering was getting them nowhere. She asked Sam to go on deck with her and watch the sunrise. They went above and walked forward and into the bows. With her elbows on the rail, her eyes dreamily on the bow wave, knifed up into foaming pink from the ink-blue water, she began to talk.

It was the first time she had voiced definite suspicions of Ben Rosen to Sam. She said she believed that the whole trouble was that his scheme, as originally planned, had gone astray—somehow.

"But I don't see what Rosen's motive would be. He

always seemed sympathetic with Porter. He fought with Mr. Baxton over that will. I was sure he wanted Porter to inherit the Baxton empire—not Ray. The simplest plan would have been to have Ray killed in some way that looked accidental, so that he could have the corpse for legal purposes. If Rosen is at the bottom of this, and if his scheme did not go astray, what is his motive?"

Sam answered: "Perhaps Rosen doesn't want Porter Baxton to inherit the Baxton empire. You've seen how he loves power and authority. Perhaps Rosen is planning to seize the corporation."

"How?"

"With no one to prove that Ray is dead or alive," Sam replied, "Porter is powerless. Rosen can take the case into the courts and keep it there for years. He could have the corporation thrown into receivership and be appointed receiver. There are a dozen schemes he could use to get control of the corporation. It's one of the biggest fortunes in America. It's enough to tempt any man. He's smart, but if he is at the bottom of this, if he's responsible for Jeff's death, I'll find it out."

Marthana said in a faint small voice: "You'd kill him!"

"I would."

She said presently: "What will we find on that island?"

"I don't know."

"Cannibals?"

"It isn't likely to be inhabited, except of course—" He hesitated.

"By whom?" Marthana said quickly.

"Some kind of gang." He didn't elaborate that. He had given it thought, but one guess was as good as another. It all depended on Ben Rosen's innocence or guilt, and, if the latter, upon what his plans were. If Ray Baxton had been kidnaped by one of the gangs which infest the South Seas, the worst in all known human nature could be expected. Wanted criminals, escaped convicts, human wolves of the sea comprised some of these gangs.

THE GOLDEN COLOR in the east brightened, and the crimson tip of the sun appeared on the horizon. The light crimsoned the tips of the blue waves. Red rays from the sun struck up into masses of cumulous clouds which looked as solid as though carved from stone; illuminated them from within in a glory of colors. It was a moment of breathless and indescribable beauty.

Marthana suddenly began to cry. She dropped her face into her hands and cried silently. Sam laid his arm gently across her shoulders and said huskily, "You'd better turn in, old timer."

She took her hands down and straightened up and looked at him, trying to smile. Her eyes were wet. Her cheeks were wet.

"I'm disgusted with myself, Sam. I'm so tired. It all seems so futile. Why are we going to this place? What are we going to find? I'll make a terrible confession to you: I'm not in love with Porter. I'm going to go through with it because I think he needs me. But I don't love him any more. After I really knew Jeff—I couldn't. I've never loved anybody in my life but Jeff."

She put her hands to her face and began to cry again, in that silent way. Sam looked grimly past her at a school of flying fish which broke just ahead of the bow, but he was unaware of their amazing grace and the silvery beauty of their return to the blue water.

He was sorry for Marthana, but there was nothing you could do for a girl who loved a man who was dead. He took her firmly by the elbow and led her aft to the stairway, and down the stairs to her room.

He opened the door upon a room flooded with rosy sunlight.

Koori, in the upper bunk, was sitting up staring with wide, alarmed eyes at the opening door.

She wore white pajamas, presumably Marthana's.

Her eyes, on Sam's green ones, were suddenly dark with terror. Her golden face was somber and mysterious. Her lashes moved lazily down to her cheeks and she smiled faintly.

Marthana said, in a choked voice: "You're such a good egg, Sam."

And he said, "You're a pretty good guy yourself. Turn in!"

He went to his room. He suspected that his present charter could lead, before it was over, to enough drama, enough trouble, to last a man a lifetime. But what he could not suspect was the mysterious and amazing and horrible way in which the future would disclose the fates of his passengers and himself.

He fell on the bunk with his clothes on, and did not wake up until supper-time.

18

THE FUNERAL

IT TOOK THE *Blue Goose,* one of the fastest trading schooners in the South Seas, ten days from Singapore to Murder Island. In that time, some of Singapore's suspicions were confirmed and some of them weren't.

When Marthana insisted that Koori was in love with him, he scoffed. In those ten days he watched the Princess of Saballa at every opportunity. Sometimes he found her looking at him softly, with her faint, alluring smile. That might have been love. But at other times he surprised in her eyes a look of cool speculation, of calculation, which always turned to wide-eyed terror when she found him scrutinizing her. He was convinced that she was lying to him, that she was involved in some way in an intrigue.

As for Ben Rosen and the personal physician of the late Oliver Baxton, Sam imperceptibly lost his suspicions. There was never much friendliness lost between him and them, and he believed that this was due to their uneasiness in a world to which they were unaccustomed. They were used to big cities. Dr. Hobb was a society man—and a woman's man. Ben Rosen was a product of American industry. Despite the comforts of the *Blue Goose,* life on a schooner was strange to them.

Sam came to believe before the voyage was over that he had misjudged them; that Dr. Hobb was merely a fish out of water, and that Ben Rosen was in a state of perpetual worry over the fate of the Baxton empire and his responsibilities.

One night he turned in early. It had been the kind of day so trying to a sailing man—a day of light and vagrant breezes, with the equatorial sun beating down, the tar going soft in the deck seams, the sails hanging with hardly a flutter for hours at a time.

A faint quartering breeze had sprung up with moonrise, but there was no body to it, and the schooner was ghosting along with hardly more than a murmur of ripples along her sides.

Undressing for bed, Sam heard a low voice above him murmur: "Do you think he suspects anything?"

It was a man's voice. It would be either the voice of the lawyer or the doctor. It was so low-pitched that it was hard to say. Scarcely more than a whisper, it was carried to Sam by the sounding-box effect of the mainsail which was swung out over that side, so slack that the sheets were almost dragging.

Another low voice answered: "No."

The first voice: "I sometimes wonder. The lengths we've gone to—"

Sam held his breath. His heart was thumping.

"He doesn't suspect anything."

"But he's so damned shrewd! It would be a pity if, after all the pains we've taken—"

"He doesn't," Ben Rosen said curtly. "Stop worrying."

The sound of footsteps, as one of the crew crossed the

deck, brought this tantalizing conversation to a close. But Sam had the proof that he wanted. Ben Rosen and Dr. Hobb were as guilty as he had suspected from the beginning.

He wondered again just what the hunchback's scheme was; what development in this baffling mystery he should be prepared for when they reached Murder Island.

On the following night, shortly before dawn, Sam was awakened by the *serang*, who said that the mate wished him to come on deck. There was land ahead. According to Rufe's reckoning, the land was Murder Island.

ON DECK, WHEN his eyes were accustomed to the night, Sam ordered sail shortened. The loom of the land, a point off the starboard bow, was far enough above water to make him suspect they were close in. The pilot's guide had little to say about Murder Island, the last reference to it was some forty years old, and in the intervening years subaqueous volcanic activity had changed some of the channels in the Spice Island group.

Murder Island rose green and mysterious from the sea with the dawn; a small island, thickly covered with tropical foliage, no more than six miles in length, mountainous in the interior.

Studying it through his glasses in the dawn light, Sam was struck by its air of brooding mystery which was explained by nothing visible. He saw no sign of habitation.

Rufe had picked up the island from the south, and they ran along it now, about two miles offshore, outside the barrier reef. There was a lagoon on the northern side, and, according to the Pacific Pilot, there was a straight, deep channel through the reef and on into the lagoon squarely centered in the northern side.

The rollers broke in a creamy froth on the barrier reef. The sun rose and Murder Island became a sinister but beautiful gem in a setting of golden cloud masses.

As the schooner, under jib alone, sailed through the passage, Sam, in the bows, trained his glasses on the shore.

What would he find here? Was Ray Baxton alive on this island, being held prisoner, as Ben Rosen suggested? Did Ben Rosen actually have some diabolically clever plan that he hoped to carry to its conclusion here? But the question that Sam wanted answered more than any other was: would the mystery surrounding the death of Jeff Carmichael be cleared up here?

He caught the gleam of a snow-white beach, a narrow strip of sand between the jade green of the lagoon and the mass of cocoanut palms which lined the circular sweep of shore. A flight of frigate birds and terns came winging out from this greenery and flew about the schooner's masts. Ashore, cocks began crowing, at first singly, in challenge, then in a growing chorus, which could only mean that the island was inhabited. The fragrance of the land, dew-drenched and sweet from the night, floated out on a mild breeze.

The bird cries, the crowing cocks, the land fragrance and all that his eyes could discern should have dispelled that sense of sinister mystery, yet it remained.

The sun came up suddenly. Darkness drained from the shadows under the cocoanut palms fringing the shore, and the ruby rays found a scattering of white houses just behind the trees.

*Sam found the body
four feet down.*

There seemed to be about a dozen of them, all white,
all with windows, some roofed with red tile, others with
thatch. These had presumably been built by the British
pearling company that had abandoned Murder Island,
after the pearls were exhausted, some fifty years ago.

One of these habitations was markedly larger than the
others, and set some distance apart; a large white house
built into the face of the hill which rose sheerly behind
the settlement.

The shouts of Willie Ru, who was casting the lead and
calling off the depths in the curious sing-song used by all
serangs, awakened the others. Ben Rosen was the first to
appear. He came forward in pajamas, dressing gown and
bedroom slippers, chewing an unlighted black cigar.

"Is this it?"

"Yes."

"Is it inhabited?"

"Yes. But I haven't seen anyone."

The hunchback stared at the shore line. "Are those white things houses?"

"Yes."

Sam was swinging the glasses along the shore. Suddenly, in a clearing near one of the houses, he saw a group of people. There were five. Two were women and three were men. The distance was so great that Sam could not distinguish their features, but he guessed that they were white. The women wore white dresses and the men wore nothing but white pants.

They were standing about a rectangular hole in the sand, into which one of the men was shoveling sand.

"What's going on?" Ben Rosen wanted to know.

Dr. Hobb came forward, asking questions as he came. Was this the island? Was Captain Shay sure? What was going on ashore? Sam answered his questions and told him to borrow Rufe's binoculars, which were 12-power.

"I think it's a burial."

THIS GUESS WAS verified a moment later when the sound of singing voices came softly across the water. They were singing "Nearer My God To Thee."

And suddenly Sam saw the woman with blue hair. She was one of the two women, and he had thought at first that her hair was white. It was not white. The rising sun suddenly brightened to flaming gold and clearly illuminated the somewhat mysterious spectacle in the clearing near the beach.

He focused the glasses on her. It should have been

an illusion. It was amazing and fantastic. Her hair was sky-blue!

Dr. Hobb returned with Rufe's binoculars. The schooner was gliding closer and closer to the shore. The doctor put the binoculars to his eyes, adjusted them and said, "Good Lord! Captain! Do you see that woman?"

"I'm looking at her."

"She's the most beautiful creature I ever saw in my life!"

Marthana came running forward, with Koori only a few steps behind her. Both girls had slipped dressing gowns over their pajamas. The blond girl cried: "Sam! Sam! What is it? What's going on?"

"They've just buried somebody."

Dr. Hobb gave Marthana the binoculars and said, in a shaking voice: "That woman with blue hair! Look at her!"

Marthana put the glasses to her eyes, looked and said breathlessly: "How utterly fantastic!"

"Isn't she beautiful?"

"I never saw hair that color in my life!"

"It's as blue as your eyes," Dr. Hobb said. "It's as blue as the sky!"

Sam glanced at him curiously. He had never seen the suave young man so agitated. Always, he had been distinguished by his air of amusement, his refusal to be excited by anything. He was now trembling. He could not get the glasses back from Marthana quickly enough. When he put them to his eyes, he said, "Damnation!" with angry disappointment. "Gone!"

They had all gone. The grave was filled and the group was vanishing among the cocoanut palms. It was surprising that they did not come down to the shore, for a ship must have been an unusual sight in this lagoon.

Sam glanced at the lawyer. Ben Rosen was smiling faintly. His air was one of utmost mystery. Sam fidgeted. Once ashore, just what did Ben Rosen intend to do? Sam was curious. He was, once again, overwhelmed by a sense of his own lack of cleverness in any competition with this brilliant lawyer.

Sam's eyes slid on, speculating, to Koori. The Princess of Saballa had said nothing. She was an island woman. She stared at Murder Island, as if estimating its capacity for trouble, for danger. Her long lashes pointed straight out, as she gazed steadily along the shore line. What Sam could see of her expression told him nothing at all. But when, suddenly, she glanced up at him, he surprised in the depths of her eyes, once again, that nameless terror. It was instantly masked. She lowered her lashes, lifted them, and her eyes were softly aglow, and there was a tender smile at her small and lovely mouth.

She said nothing. But her eyes had said enough. She knew much more about that island than she had ever intimated.

Of them all, Dr. Hobb was the most anxious to go ashore as soon as possible. His excitement continued. His eyes glowed. His face was flushed. He talked continuously. It was as if that glimpse of a woman, hundreds of feet away, had turned a key in him, unlocking him. He talked. He talked about nothing but the amazing woman with blue hair. He must see her at close range.

He said, with eagerness, to Sam: "Wasn't it your impression, Captain Shay, that she's beautiful?"

"Yes," Sam said.

"I never saw anyone in my life half so beautiful!"

Marthana said: "She's probably married, doctor, and has nine children."

"I don't believe it!" he said indignantly.

AFTER A HASTY breakfast, Sam had the cutter lowered, and Rufe and Willie Ru rowed the party ashore. Before starting, Sam gave each of the men an automatic pistol and a spare clip of shells from the arms locker. He didn't like the idea of arming Ben Rosen, yet, until the hunchback brought this fight into the open, Sam could do nothing but pretend that no battle existed.

As the cutter approached the clearing where the burial had taken place, the two women and the three men reappeared among the trees, picking their way across the white sand to the water's edge. If they had been oblivious to the schooner's presence, or if they had deliberately ignored its appearance, they had evidently decided to acknowledge it now.

They formed a line along the edge of the water and solemnly waited for the cutter. Sam, in the stern, searched their faces and was puzzled by what he saw. Under their solemnity, he believed he detected a common terror. But all five were making a determined effort to conceal it behind various expressions of reserve or unfriendliness. The blue-haired woman interested him the most.

She was beautiful and she looked respectable and refined, which was more than he could say for the rest of them. He was astonished because the gang responsible for the murder of Jeff Carmichael and the disappearance of Ray Baxton wasn't piratical in appearance. He hadn't expected refined-looking women, for example, but his suspicions weren't dissipated by what he saw.

The other woman was about thirty-five years old; a tall, lean woman who looked like a radical, with her short, straight black hair, her long jade pendants, her small, black, smoldering eyes and her thin, cruel mouth. She looked dangerous.

As for the men, two were of a size, and, even at a distance, looked startlingly alike. Both were stocky, blond and copper-colored from exposure to the sun. They were unmistakably twins. They were round-faced and blue-eyed. The hair of each was close-clipped, and the head of each was round, too. They looked sullen.

The other man was tall and elderly. His hair, too, was clipped. He was sun-browned. His thin head was covered with white stubble. His nose was hooked and his few teeth resembled fangs. He looked like a pirate. Or a turkey gobbler, with his wattles, his purplish-red nose, and his small, mean, oystery eyes.

Dr. Hobb sat in the bows, with Rufe's glasses to his eyes, staring at the blue-haired woman, and making comments as the cutter drew closer to shore. When the keel grated in sand in shoaling water, he was the first out. He jumped into the shallow water and went splashing to the white beach, as if he intended to take the blue-haired woman in his arms.

His greeting, whatever it was, resulted in no enthusiasm from the blue-haired girl or any of her companions. Unsmiling, the five of them stared at Dr. Hobb, then at the others who were coming up the beach. Once again, Sam gathered that impression of five people all trying to hide their terror behind a front of aloofness.

Sam was the last out. He followed Marthana and Koori. He was aware that this moment was tense and strange. Even with his feet solidly on the land, even with the morning sun beating on him, the palms murmuring in the trade with their sound like soft rain, the cumulous clouds piled up above the green hill like masses of rounded, dimpled masonry—with all these reassuring impressions, he could not rid himself of the feeling of mystery.

Ben Rosen was talking to the old man with the hooked nose. The hunchback was taking prompt advantage of an opportunity to show his authority.

"What place is this?"

The man with the hooked nose and the fangs slowly and coldly answered, in a voice as deep and resonant as a voice in a cistern: "It is called Murder Island."

Ben Rosen, perhaps angered by his coolness, said pompously: "Who's in charge here?"

"Manuel Karlov," the old man drawled, still with that air of cold reserve, and this was emphasized by the attitudes of his four companions. Their faces were unsmiling, unwelcoming.

"Where is he?" Ben Rosen barked.

The old man inclined his head toward the large white building set into the face of the hill.

"He cannot be disturbed."

The hunchback's face was flushed with resentment. "Why not?" he said impatiently.

The blue-haired girl answered in a sweet, low voice: "He will see no one, ever, until four in the afternoon."

Sam heard Dr. Hobb's gasp, and supposed it was the

doctor's response to the clear beauty of that remarkable woman's voice.

BEN ROSEN LOOKED more and more indignant. He looked as if these rebuffs were intended as personal affronts. "Why not?" he said again.

"He is writing his autobiography," the black-haired woman answered.

Ben Rosen had snatched a cigar out of his white coat and savagely bit into the end of it. He tried another attack. He said, in a softer voice: "Didn't someone die?"

"Yes," the blue-haired girl said quietly, and looked swiftly at the sea. She was fascinating. Her skin was milk-white, as white as her dress, which was of cotton, a simple dress that bore out the distant promise of a slender and perfect body. Her eyes were the pure blue of Ceylon sapphires. The blue eyes, with her milk-white skin, made her blue hair even more startling. Her face was slim and beautifully modeled, her delicately curving lips a soft pink.

"Well," the hunchback said impatiently, "who died?"

"One of us," the blue-haired girl answered without looking at him. It was as if they had been instructed to say as little as possible.

Marthana was studying her critically, with the friendly half-smile a tolerant woman will wear when she sees another woman reach for and achieve artistic perfection. The blue hair was amazing. As blue as the tropical sky, it was fine and lustrous, parted in the middle and drawn straight back to expose small, perfect ears. A single braid was wound once about the girl's head, giving the effect of a coronet.

Marthana realized that the blue-haired girl was a

masterpiece of exotic allurement. The milk-white skin was lovely. The blue eyes were amazing. The blue hair and the contrasting white dress, so simple, so demurely revealing, were sensational.

Sam's first impression persisted: She was the only respectable-looking one of the lot. The other woman, at close range, was even more sinister. She used mascara freely to intensify the darkness of her eyes. There was something about her that reminded Sam of a predatory bird. Perhaps it was her thin nose, or the small, thin, hungry-looking mouth. Her hands were thin but they looked powerful.

She looked at Sam's red hair. And he had the impression that she hated him.

"Who died?" Sam said, watching her eyes.

"A man named Mace Littlejohn," she answered. She looked as if she were about to say more, but had thought better of it. It was baffling and irritating. He again had the feeling that something was happening here beneath the surface, or that something was about to happen.

Sam shifted his eyes to the two young men who looked alike. He guessed their age at about thirty. They looked so much alike that they must be twins. Of the five, their attitude was the more frankly hostile. Their blue eyes glared. Their identical mouths were set sullenly. They even stood alike, with legs apart, fists on stocky hips. Tweedle-Dee and Tweedle-Dum, Sam thought with fleeting amusement. Their resemblance to those famous brothers was remarkable.

The old man, with his closely-clipped white hair, his beak of a nose, his four or five remaining fangs, wore a poker face. It had the texture of oiled leather. His eyes were uneasy rather than hostile.

Studying them, Sam decided that if Ben Rosen knew them, he was concealing it perfectly.

The twin on the left suddenly said: "Visitors—"

And the other twin finished: "—are not welcome here."

Their voices were identical. Each quivered with antagonism.

"If you wish water—" the one on the left began another sentence.

"—you can have water," the other finished it.

It made Sam and Marthana exchange quick glances, but they would learn that the Ringrose twins always spoke in this fashion; that the communion between them was so complete that their thoughts generally followed the same channel.

SAM WAS CURIOUS about that burial, but it was obvious that these people resented questions.

He said briskly: "We've come here to look for a man who was lost off a ship about a month ago."

"Five weeks," Dr. Hobb amended, addressing the blue-haired girl.

"We have reason to believe he is on this island," Ben Rosen added pompously. He looked as if he would have relished an argument.

None of the five spoke. They looked at him blankly. Then Sam saw the blue-haired girl looking at Dr. Hobb, speculatively, sizing him up, as if his suave good looks intrigued her.

"The man," Sam said sharply, sliding his green eyes along

their unresponsive faces, "is Ray Baxton, Oliver Baxton's foster son and his heir."

The twins glanced quickly at each other. The two women exchanged a glance.

"The automobile manufacturer? Baxton Motors?" the old man asked in his deep, resonant voice.

"Yes," Sam said. "He vanished from his yacht in the Strait of Karimata on May sixth."

"We think he came here," Dr. Hobb said.

"We know he came here," the lawyer said emphatically.

"No one has been here in months," the blue-haired woman said. "If anyone came here, we'd know it. This place is small. The only water on the island is a spring just over that hill. If anyone came ashore here that long ago, we'd have seen him."

She spoke breathlessly. Her eyes flitted about uneasily as she talked. Sam knew she was lying. They were all lying. They were all pretending. So this was the gang! Not a typical gang of South Sea Island scum, cutthroats, runaway convicts, pirates, but these mystifying and hostile Americans! Smoothies!

Ben Rosen turned and looked at him meaningly.

"You don't mind, do you," Sam said, "if we stay here long enough to search the island?"

"We mind," the old man said, "but we can't stop you. We came here to be away from such people as you."

"That isn't true," the blue-haired girl said with spirit. "We came here to get away from mobs. I think we're all being ridiculous. These people are in trouble. If we can help them, we should."

The old man tightened his lips and glared at her. The

blue-haired girl looked as if she were suddenly about to cry. Her large sapphire eyes misted; her chin quivered.

"But how can we help them?" she wailed. "We're as help-less ourselves as so many sheep! One after another—" She stopped. She clenched her hands and stared desolately at the handsome doctor.

The black-haired woman cried with passion: "We ought to thank God they're here! We're the ones that need help! Why make any more of a mystery of it? Isn't it mystery enough without—" She checked herself again. It was a trick of hers, Sam would find, of leaving a sentence unfin-ished, just as the twins made a habit of completing each other's thoughts.

She was looking intently at Sam.

"The man you saw us burying was Mace Littlejohn, the poet. He was killed! He was murdered!" Her voice grew more and more hysterical. "He was killed last night outside his house, and we don't know—we haven't the faintest idea who or what it was that killed him! He—"

19

THE DEAD MAN

THEY WERE ALL talking at once, and the terror that Sam had seen in their eyes and which they had been trying to conceal was being volubly discussed if not lucidly explained. The blue-haired girl was babbling at Dr. Hobb. The twins were vehemently talking to Marthana, Koori and Rufe Pound. The old man was talking in his deep voice, now booming, to Ben Rosen. And the black-haired woman was addressing herself shrilly to Sam.

He could not hear enough of what she was saying to piece together a coherent narrative. He gathered that some unknown creature—animal, man, monster, God knew what—lived somewhere in the jungle fastnesses of the island, or in one of the caves with which the southern side of the island was honeycombed, and that it had come into the settlement late last night and horribly killed this man Mace Littlejohn; but that this was not the mysterious and unknown beast's first killing; that it had, four months previously, killed this woman's brother, and two months previous to that, Karlov's fifteen-year-old daughter.

"We have never seen it, or heard it," the black-haired woman said. "It comes and it pounces. It—it strangles them. It clutches their throats in its—" She stopped, staring at Sam with widened, terrified eyes. "It is utterly horrible. It crushes their necks—every bone."

"Gorilla," Sam guessed.

"Its tracks are not a gorilla's, or any ape's," she disagreed. "I'll show you. None of us has ever seen or heard of tracks like them, and Karlov has hunted in Sumatra, India and Africa. He has never seen or heard of tracks like them. Just a straight line, like a—"

The old man's booming voice drowned her out. "No, no. It leaves nothing but this horrible odor, like dead flesh— like a tiger's breath."

"It isn't a tiger," the blue-haired woman declared, and her voice was thin and high with hysteria. "You can see the tracks, by Mace's house."

One of the twins began: "But the worst is that it comes back—"

And the other finished: "And digs up the bodies and strips the bones!"

Marthana shivered. "Oh, not really!"

The twins chorused: "The night after the burial!"

Sam said firmly: "Let's have a look at the tracks."

The black-haired woman led the way through the palms and past three of the white coral houses to a small house which stood in a little clearing of its own. No vegetation grew there; sand was all about.

Near the front door, in the sand, were splotches of blood, dried and black. And just in front of the door was an area of blood, about a yard in diameter, where a violent struggle had taken place. There were the marks of a man's feet, kicking this way and that, and just behind this small area were long, narrow marks in the sand.

"Those!" the black-haired woman said with a shudder.

Sam stared at them. He had hunted in India and Sumatra and smaller islands, and he had never seen the tracks of any beast even remotely comparable to these. There were no toe marks. The track was about fourteen inches in length by no more than two in width, and the width from end to end did not vary.

These tracks approached the house from inland, and they vanished in the same direction, although it was impossible to say which set of tracks was which. He estimated the length of this unknown creature's stride at slightly more than that of a very tall man's normal stride.

From the tracks it was impossible to say whether the creature walked on one pair of legs or on all fours, or to make any kind of guess regarding its height or weight.

He said: "I never saw or heard of anything like it anywhere in this part of the world—or any other part."

The blue-haired girl was saying: "It must come in absolute silence. We've never heard it. Last night was utterly still. There wasn't a breath of air. I was awake. I was reading when I heard Mace scream. It was so hideous that I almost fainted. I have a small hunting rifle which we sometimes use for sharks. I snatched it up and ran out. There was this dreadful smell in the air—like rotting flesh! Mace was lying here, all crumpled and bleeding, and his neck was crushed—just crushed! Not broken, but smashed and mangled!"

"Any kind of marks?" Sam asked.

"Yes. Five marks. Four on one side and one on the other. But it could not have been a human hand. No human hand in the world was ever strong enough to crush a strong man's neck like that. Mace was a powerful man. He was over six feet tall, and built like an athlete. He had shoulders as wide as yours, and a neck as strong as yours. His neck was just crushed."

"You could see fragments of the backbone," the old man said. "Broken and crushed."

KOORI HAD KNELT down beside one of the tracks. When she stood up, Sam saw the same terror in her eyes that was in the other's.

He said: "Koori, have you ever seen or heard of anything like this?"

She answered: "Vaguely. Long ago, when I was a little girl, I heard of some monster on Borneo that came out of the jungle and killed the tribesmen. But it ate them. It pulled their heads off and drank their blood. But we were sure it was a gigantic orang-outang that had gone mad."

"This comes back on the second night," the black-haired woman said, trembling. "It strips the bones. It stripped my brother's bones. It tore his skeleton apart and took every shred of flesh."

It was too fantastic for Sam. He tried to picture a beast built like a man, a throwback, or a result of cross-breeding, or some survivor of a prehistoric day, but his imagination failed. In his seven years in these waters, he had heard many strange, fantastic stories. He was a canny, level-headed young man. He was skeptical of any tale dealing with the supernatural. He had been skeptical of the existence of a monster which, according to old legend, lived in a lagoon and attacked and devoured men. He had, in fact, chartered his schooner to a scientist who wanted to investigate this monster, and had found to his surprise and horror that the monster existed, and that it did destroy and devour men according to the legend. He had had a hand in destroying what proved to be a gigantic amoeba, a unicellular organism which had grown, over a period of centuries, to an incredible size.

Yet his natural skepticism remained unshaken. He thought it was a cooked-up story.

He said to the blue-haired girl: "What did you see?"

"Absolutely nothing."

"There was a moon," he pointed out.

"It was brilliant moonlight," she affirmed. "I must have been here within two minutes after Mace screamed. I expected to find him with his neck crushed, just as Anita's brother's had been, and just as Lolita Karlov's had been. I mean, I was prepared for that, and I wanted a shot at the thing. But there was nothing here but Mace and the tracks."

"I came out only a moment later," the woman with the bobbed black hair said. "And so did the twins. We have only the one rifle, but we wasted no time. We followed the tracks to the hill, where they vanished in the thick grass. It was useless trying to follow them in the night. And we were horribly shaken."

Dr. Hobb said: "It must have long-fingered paws as strong as steel. It simply clasps the neck of its victim in one of these paws, and crushes it to a pulp, bones and all."

"Exactly," the old man said.

"When was the first killing?" the hunchback asked.

"About six months ago. That was Lolita Karlov."

"Nuts," Sam said. All conversation was suspended. Every pair of eyes turned to him. "Where's that shovel?"

The old man answered: "The one I dug the grave with?"

"Yeah."

"Behind my house."

"That one?"

"Yes."

"Rufe, get that shovel."

The old man said excitedly, "What for?"

"We're going to dig this guy up."

The bobbed-haired woman cried passionately, "Oh, no!"

"Rufe, snap into it!"

Rufe departed for the shovel. The black-haired woman, with hands on hips, eyes blazing, thrust her face close to Sam's. "I'd like to know," she panted, "what right you have to disturb our privacy!"

"The answer to that, lady, is that we've got as much right on this island as you have. This island belongs to the Dutch. By the way, have you got a permit to be here?"

The bobbed-haired woman retreated from the harshness of his tone, but she continued to stare at him as if she would have liked to murder him. She didn't answer him. No one answered him.

"I'd like to see it," the red-haired man went on. "I'd like to see the date on it."

"We have no permit," she snapped, "but that's beside the point. You have no right coming here and digging up our dead!"

Ben Rosen said suddenly: "I think she's right, Captain Shay!"

Sam looked at him curiously. "Do you?" he drawled.

"And you can stop getting tough!" the hunchback said angrily.

"I'm not getting tough," Sam answered. "I am tough. Marthana, if anybody tries to stop us digging that guy up, shoot 'em full of holes."

"Okay," Marthana said tensely.

RUFE HAD APPEARED with the shovel. Sam left the group and he and Rufe went to the clearing where the grave was. Everyone followed.

Sam began to shovel sand out of the hole. He went about it coolly and methodically. He didn't hate or fear the dead. He'd seen too many, and he had a strong stomach. He found the body four feet down, wrapped in canvas. Without compunction or hesitation, he lifted out the corpse and unrolled the canvas.

It was that of a man of about forty, a large, powerful man with a slightly bald, graying head.

Everyone turned after one glance, or began to move away. Even Marthana, who was a brave girl, didn't want more than one look.

The neck was as they had described it—horribly crushed. Sam could easily see the marks of the beast—four on the right side of the neck and one on the left—great, deep marks of fingers more powerful than Sam had supposed existed. Tissue and bones had been crushed and crumpled by that superhuman hand, crushed to a pulp.

Sam said briskly: "Come on, doc. You're an expert."

Dr. Hobb came over with an expression of distaste. He knelt down. He turned the body this way and that for a better examination of the crushed and contused flesh.

Sam looked up at him. "What do you think, doc?"

"This was certainly enough to kill him."

The bobbed-haired woman said harshly: "Good God, are you still skeptical?"

"Find out how this guy was killed, doc."

"But I don't think there's any question about it."

"Did you ever perform any autopsies?"

"Hundreds. But I can't perform one here without laboratory equipment. What do you suspect?"

"That maybe this fellow died of other causes."

"My opinion is that he died of strangulation. Look at his eyes, and his tongue, and the color of his flesh. That's enough for me. It would be enough for any medical examiner in the world."

"Are you convinced now?" the bobbed-haired woman said.

"I'll answer that this way," Sam answered. "There's something so phony about all this that I could cut it with a knife. Bury this guy, Rufe. We're through with him."

"Okay, skipper."

"So we're phony," the woman said in a menacing voice.

Rufe and Willie Ru returned the mangled victim to its grave and began to fill the grave again.

"Well," Sam answered, "we've come here, as I told you, looking for a man who was lost off a yacht five weeks ago. We know he's on this island. You're all lying. What's the answer?"

"That you're a fool!" she cried. "You're a blundering fool!"

"Captain," the lawyer said irritably, "you're not accomplishing anything with these strong-arm methods."

"They're the only methods I've got, mister. Ray Baxton is on this island. We know he is on this island. These people know it. Why should we use kid gloves on a gang like this?"

"Captain—" Dr. Hobb began threateningly. He was standing close to the blue-haired girl, as if he would protect her. But when Sam glanced at him, the doctor subsided.

"We figure," Sam went on, "that Ray Baxton is being held by these people for ransom. Why should we beat about the bush?"

The blue-haired girl said tremulously: "Captain, I swear to you, we don't know anything about a man coming to this island."

Sam looked at her. "Do you know anything about a man leaving this island? Maybe a month ago. A big, powerful guy about my age and four inches taller, with shoulders like a bull. Dark hair, a big mouth. He wore a white silk shirt, a dark red sash and blue velvet pants. He looked like an artist."

The blue-haired girl cried: "Chester Cave! That was Chester Cave! He deserted us about a month ago! He took our only boat."

"Ah!" Sam said, as if it were important. "So you haven't got a boat."

"You heard her!" the twins chorused sullenly.

"Rufe," said Sam. "Willie. Check up on that. They say they haven't a boat. Find out. Go around the island. You go north, Rufe, and you go south, Willie. Look for a boat. Any kind."

"Okay, skipper."

When they had gone, Sam said: "Tell me some more about this Chester Cave."

And the snag-toothed man snarled: "That's all we know."

"Ask Karlov!" the bobbed-haired woman cried.

"Sure! While I'm gone, find out something about this gang, Marthana."

"Okay, skipper."

20

THE ARTISTS

SAM STRODE OFF through the palms toward the large white house set in the face of the hill. He had already informed himself that it contained three windows and a door on the front, all barred, and that all the windows on the sides were likewise covered with strong-looking bars.

Sam went to the door. It wasn't unlikely that Ray Baxton, if a prisoner of these people, was a prisoner inside this house which, with its thick coral walls and barred windows and door, was a veritable fortress.

He banged on the bars with the butt of his automatic pistol. Beyond the bars, a foot away, was a heavy wooden inner door made of planks and thick, wide iron straps, badly rusted.

The door was opened by a tall, skinny man in blue dungarees. He looked like a ghost. The skin was drawn tight over his high cheekbones, and his eyes glimmered in sunken sockets.

"Are you Karlov?"

"No. I am Karlov's servant."

"Tell Karlov I want to see him."

The death's head expression did not change. The eyes glimmered at him neither with curiosity nor hostility.

"Karlov sees no one until after four o'clock."

"Tell him it is important."

"There is no use. He will not see you."

"Tell him—" Sam began, but the door was closed slowly, firmly, in his face.

Sam returned to the others in time to hear Marthana saying, in a friendly voice to the blue-haired girl: "How long have you been here?"

The blue-haired girl answered: "A little over a year."

Sam sensed that his going had removed a great deal of restraint. He was aware, too, that the blue-haired woman and the tall, handsome doctor were eyeing each other with a mutual fascination.

"I suppose," she said, as Sam came up behind Marthana, "you're curious to know what we're doing here—rather, why we're here."

"Very curious," Dr. Hobb said softly, and his voice was that of a man ensnared.

"See him?" Marthana asked.

"No," Sam said. "The door has bars on it."

"We came here," the blue-haired girl said dreamily, "to escape civilization."

"The machine age and all that it represents," the old turkey gobbler said in his deep, rain-barrel voice, and looked at Sam belligerently, as if Sam were a personal and highly offensive representative of the machine age.

"The money lust and the greed," the old fellow went on, with that antagonistic air. "The Hitlers and the Mussolinis and the Stalins, and the imperialists generally, and the machines that rot a man's soul, and the stinking, self-seeking politicians!"

"We came to be free!" the blue-haired girl cried with shining eyes.

"And are you free?" Dr. Hobb asked.

She stared at him. "Free? Of course we're free!"

"You're from the States, of course?"

"Yes. From New York."

BEN ROSEN SAID softly, "What have you here to take the place of the thrill that accompanies living the modern pace?"

"Peace and calm," she answered, "and the chance to express ourselves!"

"How do you express yourself?"

The blue-haired woman said: "She is Anita Mendoza. She is a clever sculptor. My name is Faustine Fife. I am an artist. This"—she indicated the old man—"is Hiram Fillow. He is an artist. Jeremy and Jorrel Ringrose are playwrights."

The hunchback looked at them, in turn, as Faustine Fife introduced them. "Do you do your work for money or for posterity?"

Hiram Fillow shouted: "For ourselves! We are untainted by any commercial—"

"Trot out some of your work," Singapore said quietly. "Yours, Miss Fife? And yours, Miss Mendoza?"

Their eyes swung to his face.

"You don't believe we're what we say we are!" the bobbed-haired woman shrilled.

"Lady," Sam said, "I have to be shown." He turned on the twins. "How about you? Playwrights. Are you doing a play?"

They said, "Yes!" belligerently. Each thrust out his jaw.

"For whom?" Ben Rosen jeered.

"Ourselves!"

"But who will act in it?"

"We are not—" Jeremy began.

"—interested in that," Jorrel finished.

"Amazing!" said Ben Rosen. "A play not intended for the stage! A play the lines of which will never be spoken by actors! But what's the pleasure of it?"

"To satisfy ourselves," the twins answered.

Sam looked at them with a hard grin. "This," he said, "gets better and better. And this bird Karlov—he's writing his autobiography?"

"Yes!" the twins shouted.

"For whom?" Ben Rosen said.

"Himself!"

"An autobiography," Ben Rosen stated, "is nothing but a breakdown of an ego that simply can't contain itself any longer. It must burst out upon the world. What is the satisfaction of writing your autobiography for yourself alone?"

"Ask Karlov," the old man boomed.

Sam said, "Let's get going, now. I want to see some of this self-expression."

The bobbed-haired woman with the jade ear pendants said harshly: "You have no right—"

The lovely girl with the blue hair interrupted. "Wait, Anita. The gentleman wants proof that we're what we say we are. We aren't, of course, obliged to prove anything. But the sooner they find out everything they want to know, the sooner they will leave us to ourselves." She looked at Sam, her cheeks flushing delicately. "Nothing that we've done," she said tremulously, "was intended for any eyes but our own. We often don't show our work to each other. That's entirely the point. We don't care whether our work is seen or not."

She looked appealingly at Dr. Hobb, so tall, so handsome, so civilized in his perfect-fitting whites. And Sam wondered again about this strange passion that had sprung up so spontaneously between the two.

The bobbed-haired woman said scornfully to Sam: "You wouldn't know art if it came up and bit you on the leg!"

"No," Sam admitted heartily, "but I'd know honesty if it came up and looked me in the eye!"

She sneered: "Ah, yes; I know you now! The great strong man of the open spaces—so brutally frank!"

He gave her a one-sided grin.

Faustine Fife said with dignity, "Please. Let's get this over with."

21

BUT IS IT ART?

THEY FOLLOWED FAUSTINE Fife into the small cottage she occupied. Like the other houses, it was built of slabs of white coral. The masonry was neat, and the construction would withstand any wind that blew, hurricane or typhoon.

The interior consisted of a single room, which was neat and unquestionably feminine. Small canvases were arranged about the walls. One was a black smear of paint with lightning-like zig-zags of vivid green intersecting it. Near the center was a blob of blood-red paint, and on the fringe were purple waves.

The blue-haired woman was like a little girl, self-conscious and shy. This, she said, was the soul of Stalin, the dictator of Russia. Another was called the Fundamental Whirl of Life. It looked like a pinwheel. Bright colors—yellow and red, blue and green—spiralled outward symmetrically from a core of sickly yellow.

"That's my conception of life," the girl said. "Life is a whirl—mostly a horrible, dizzying whirl. I simply tried to set down what I felt."

"Is life," Singapore asked dryly, "a horrible, dizzying whirl on Murder Island?"

Her blue eyes slid quickly to him. Her hands fluttered as if, for a moment, her nerves were out of control.

"Life," she said, "would be perfect if that thing that is killing us could be killed."

Sam turned to the twins. "What's this play of yours all about?"

"The last hours—"

"—of Socrates."

He looked at Miss Mendoza. "How about your stuff?"

She glared at him. "My 'stuff'—" she began shrilly.

"Anita," Faustine Fife said quietly. "Please. Show him."

Anita Mendoza said bitterly, "Very well. Come on."

Her house was not far from the blue-haired girl's. Her work was in clay. Little as Sam knew about such things, it was typical of the woman. It was both sinister and revolting. There were monstrous frogs, lizards and snakes made of clay and painted hideous colors. As far as he was concerned, the corner of her room devoted to her work was a chamber of horrors.

Dr. Hobb said, "They're tremendously interesting, Miss Mendoza." It was evident that the personal physician of the late Oliver Baxton did not approve of Sam's bluntness in dealing with these people.

They went now to see Hiram Fillow's work, and Sam went along, hoping for clues. Clues to confirm his suspicions that they were lying. It was his belief that this amazing colony had been established on this island not more than two months ago, as part of a thoroughly engineered plan to kidnap Ray Baxton and hold him for ransom, the largest ransom ever known, probably. Perhaps they were artists and perhaps they were not. The only one who surprised him was the blue-haired girl. She was beautiful and gentle, and his opinion that she was respectable persisted. But the rest of them were crooks. And he still didn't believe the fantastic story about the beast who came silently out of the jungle and strangled its victims.

He would ask Marthana later what she thought about their art. It didn't matter much, anyhow.

The work of Hiram Fillow was in a class with the strange paintings of Miss Fife. He called himself a neo-impressionist.

The old turkey gobbler's house was untidy. Piles of old magazines stood about, and the floor was littered with old paint tubes, discarded brushes and paint rags. Sam picked up newspapers and magazines and looked at the dates. They were all dated a little over a year ago.

Marthana came over and took his arm. "Let's get out of here."

"Is it art?" Sam asked.

"Dr. Hobb thinks so."

"What do you think?"

"Well," she said, "perhaps it's just as well they're isolated on this island." She frowned. "But it's obvious that they're not just pretending to be artists. Those things, crazy as they are, show skill and experience."

"Score two for them," Sam said thoughtfully.

OUTSIDE, FAUSTINE FIFE pointed out the communal eating place, a small thatched pavilion near the beach. Everyone but Manuel Karlov ate here, Hiram Fillow explained. Karlov lived and ate alone. "He has a servant," the old man added.

Miss Fife looked uneasy. She was explaining to the

doctor, in a tense voice, that they lived exclusively on the natural foods of the island. She kept twining her fingers together in a quick, nervous gesture.

Sam smoked a cigarette, listened, and let his eyes wander about. The hunchback came over to him, chewing one of his inevitable black, unlighted cigars.

"Well, how about it, captain?"

"They're as phony as the billboard on a dime museum," Sam answered. "What did you expect?"

"A gang of cutthroats."

"You'll find they're plenty tough. And it's going to be a waiting game, mister. How much dough are you prepared to fork out for Ray Baxton?"

"Plenty."

"And this Karlov is going to be plenty tough."

"We'd better take one of these empty houses," Rosen said.

"You'll be safer on the schooner."

"I'm tired of ships. We can fix ourselves up comfortably here. How can there possibly be any danger? I don't believe the story of this fabulous monster any more than you do, captain. We are here to negotiate for the delivery of Ray Baxton."

"All right, mister. We'll move ashore."

Dr. Hobb and the blue-haired girl were making their way back through the palms to her house. Sam said to Marthana, "He's fallen for her like a ton of bricks."

"Why not?" Marthana said. "He never saw anything like her before in his life! That blue hair! The mystery of her! Who wouldn't fall for her?"

"I wouldn't," Sam said. "What's the answer to that blue hair?"

"Her hair turned white prematurely, and she dyed it blue. She can't be more than twenty-three."

They set about the selection of a house with rooms enough to accommodate all of them—Marthana, Koori, Sam, the lawyer and the doctor. Ah Fat would come ashore, Sam decided, to do the cooking. Rufe Pound and Willie Ru would act as sentries, each taking a six-hour watch to cover the time from sunset to sunrise.

Rufe and Willie Ru returned from their circuit of the island at a little after mid-afternoon, to report that no boat of any description had been found. They had searched every likely hiding-place.

Sam sent them to the schooner to fetch bedding and supplies. The house selected had built-in bunks. There was a room for Marthana and Koori, another room for the lawyer and the doctor. Sam would share the room in which his sentries would sleep in the daytime.

With the exception of Faustine, who was talking to the doctor, the little band of artists watched these preparations with resentful eyes. They retired to their own houses, coming out occasionally to watch and talk indignantly among themselves.

Shortly before four o'clock, Karlov's servant came into the house where Sam was supervising the disposal of supplies. Seen in the open, he was even more strange than Sam had thought when viewing him through the barred door. He was a living skeleton—a tall, cadaverous man with a head that was a death's head, with deeply sunken eyes, with yellow parchment-like skin stretched so tightly over the bones of his face that it seemed to hold his thin, cracked lips apart. He might have been of any nationality. He had bulging joints and hands like claws. He was totally bald.

He said, in a croaking voice: "My master requests your presence at tea. All of you are to come."

"When?"

"Immediately."

22

SAM GETS TOUGH

MANUEL KARLOV WAS seated at a desk in a large gloomy room when his guests were ushered in by the manservant. It was the first room off the long corridor which ran straight through into the recesses of the house from the barred door.

The man at the desk was writing with a quill pen which he dipped from time to time into a pewter inkpot. The desk was covered with scrawled sheets of paper.

Manuel Karlov did not stop writing. His pen flew across the page. He did not look up. It was as if he were so preoccupied that he was unaware of the shuffling of feet and the voice of his servant. He thrust the pen, with its white plume, into a pewter box of shot, turned suddenly, brushed his hands together and stood up.

He was a tall man of about thirty-five, with curly black hair and a black spade beard. The whiteness of his skin testified that he seldom if ever ventured into the tropical sun which beat upon this remote island. His eyes were blue and, in this gloom, dazzling. He might have been older than thirty-five. The spade beard made it hard to say. There was no question, however, that he was a powerful man. He had powerful-looking shoulders, and large, strong hands.

Although he had turned suddenly from his occupation, there was a slow deliberateness about him that Sam Shay found sinister. In fact, there was nothing about the man or his setting that was not somehow sinister.

There were shades at the windows, and these were drawn to the bottom, so that the only light in the room was that admitted through the cracks at the bottom of the shades. It was an atmosphere befitting the man. His eyes looked more than a little mad, although the blaze Sam saw in them might have been the fires of creation.

His piercing blue eyes swept the circle of faces. He did not smile. He had thin, cruel lips, very red against the black beard, and a bulbous nose. He looked foreign.

He spoke in a deep, nasal voice, with a slight accent: "I am Manuel Karlov. You will be seated, please."

Sam glanced sharply at Ben Rosen, then at Koori, but detected nothing. Both were staring at the man with the spade beard with fascination.

The hunchback said importantly: "My name is Ben Rosen, Mr. Karlov. I am the head of the legal staff of the Baxton Corporation."

Karlov stared at him intently. "The Baxton automobile?"

"Yes, sir," the lawyer answered, and Sam suspected that the "sir" slipped out unintentionally.

"You are a long way from your factory," Karlov said, but he said it with no humor, merely as a statement of fact.

"Please sit down." He glanced at the others. He looked a long time at Koori and Marthana, scarcely paused at Dr. Hobb, and looked longest and most searchingly at Sam.

He might have been a famous doctor, a surgeon, impatiently looking over a roomful of patients, hoping to find an interesting case among them.

"You may serve tea, Cassius."

SAM SCRUTINIZED THE desk, Karlov, the floor, the ceiling, the windows and the doorway. The walls were more than two feet thick. He wondered how deep the house went into the face of the hill. He suspected that this house had been the overseer's at the time when the British were pearling here, and that it had been the repository for the pearls. It had been built as strong as this because, back in those days, pirates had been a menace to consider. He did not doubt that this house had rooms enough to accommodate the entire pearling colony, and he suspected there were underground passages and secret rooms.

He knew that Karlov was aware of his interest, was probably doing a good job of reading his mind, but the man with the spade beard seemed to pay little attention to him.

When Cassius brought tea to Karlov, the black-bearded man opened a drawer of his desk and removed a bottle containing a deep purple liquid. This, Sam knew, was a very old and very rare Javanese *arrack*. Karlov poured a generous amount into his tea and drank the tea greedily. The piercing blue eyes returned to Ben Rosen's flushed face.

"You are traveling on pleasure, I presume? That is your yacht I can see in the lagoon?"

"No," Rosen said. "She's under charter. We're here looking for Ray Baxton, the son of Oliver Baxton. He was lost off the Baxton yacht Victory five weeks ago, and we have reasons to believe he is on this island."

The man with the black spade beard and the amazingly white skin said, "Ah, really?" in a polite murmur, and Sam knew that the piercing blue eyes were minutely aware of the slightest motion in the room. Here, obviously, was a dangerous man very much on guard.

"Yes," Rosen said. "A man contacted us in Singapore with a chart of this island."

"Might he not have been an impostor?"

"No, Mr. Karlov. It is impossible for anyone to have had information of Ray Baxton's disappearance unless there was some scheme or plan or plot—some kidnap plot, perhaps."

"Amazing!" Karlov murmured. "And this fellow who contacted you, as you say—who was he?"

"These people say he was the man who deserted from here a month or so ago—Chester Cave."

"Ah! Really?"

Sam was beginning to feel restless. He liked direct action. He saw no advantage in wasting time being polite to a rogue.

"You have my consent," Karlov said, "to remain and search our island."

"When," Sam drawled, "did you buy it from Holland?"

"I beg your pardon!" Karlov said stiffly.

"I asked you when you bought this island. It used to belong to Holland. I didn't know she'd sold it."

The black-bearded man stared at him with those dazzling blue eyes. "It is our island," he answered deliberately, "by right of possession. But I give you the right to search it, if you wish."

"Nuts," Sam said.

"Captain Shay!" the hunchback said, angrily.

"And nuts to you, too," Captain Shay snapped. "Why

waste time jockeying around with this crook? He's got Ray Baxton here. We know it. He knows we know it. Get down to cases."

THERE WAS A slight movement behind Sam. The Ringrose twins had walked slowly behind his chair and now stood there.

"If you please—" Karlov began heavily.

"Listen," Sam said. "You've got Ray Baxton or you haven't got Ray Baxton. Ben Rosen represents the Baxton Corporation. Make your dicker with him. Stop wasting time."

Manuel Karlov stared at Sam, and Sam looked at Manuel Karlov. The dazzling, slightly mad blue eyes locked with the hard green ones. They stayed locked. And Karlov said, in a steely voice: "And who are you, may I ask?"

"I'm Captain Shay, of the schooner *Blue Goose.*"

"I had perhaps better inform you that it is extremely unwise to be untactful with Manuel Karlov."

"Nuts!"

The thin lips tightened. The piercing blue eyes narrowed and hardened.

"I am extremely sorry, Mr. Rosen, that I can be of no assistance to you. If Ray Baxton is on this island, he is here entirely without my knowledge. I assure you that you will be welcome here as long as you wish to stay."

The hunchback said effusively: "Thank you, Mr. Karlov, thank you. And I want to apologize for the rudeness of this young man."

"Don't bother," Sam said.

"You may see me any day after four in the afternoon."

Karlov bowed. The interview, the audience, was over.

Outside, Ben Rosen said angrily: "Captain, was that necessary? That man is dangerous. He may be more than a little crazy."

"Like a fox," Sam said.

"It was absolutely unnecessary and uncalled for—those insults!"

"Why?" Sam asked. "He's a crook. He's got Ray Baxton. He wants money for him."

"You did not have to offend him. It may complicate matters. This is a very delicate situation."

"Listen, big shot. If that guy has Ray Baxton, he wants to sell him to you for about ten million dollars. What's delicate about that?"

Dr. Hobb said sternly: "Your rudeness was uncalled for!"

Marthana took Sam's arm and said: "Come on and take a walk, gorilla. I want to talk to you alone."

They walked to the beach and sat down on a fallen palm trunk.

"Well?" she said.

"He's tough," Sam said musingly. "And he's got things corked up here as tight as a bottle of hundred-year-old brandy. I'll bet a dime he never stirs out of that house. I'll bet another dime you or me or anybody else will never get a chance to be alone with him. Did you see the way those twins came sliding up the minute I got tough?"

"I did. The question is, is Ray Baxton in that house?"

"No, it isn't," Sam disagreed. "The question is, is Ray Baxton on this island? I think he is. But if he isn't, this Karlov knows the answer."

"What are you going to do in either case?"

"Find out! If he's here, we're going to get him—without paying one dollar! If he isn't, I'm going to make Karlov talk."

"You can't."

"No?" Sam turned and looked at her. "Listen, sister. There was a guy in Singapore one time who stole something belonging to a pal of mine. We couldn't make him talk either—for a long time. We tried to lot of things. He was pretty smart. He had a trick of making himself faint whenever he wanted to."

"So what did you do?"

"We tied him up in a cargo net and swung a cargo boom overside with a block on the end of it and a rope running inboard to a winch."

"You dunked him!"

"Sure! Until a big harbor octopus came along and wrapped himself around that guy in the cargo net. How quick, after that, did we find out what we wanted?"

23

SAM PLAYS THE LOVER

IMMEDIATELY AFTER SUPPER, Sam slipped out of the house and into the tropical dusk on an expedition of inquiry. He had seen Dr. Hobb slip out a few minutes previously, but he was not particularly interested in the handsome young physician. Nor was he surprised or alarmed or particularly interested when, under a large breadfruit tree, he came upon Dr. Hobb and the blue-haired girl standing perhaps a foot apart, looking into each other's face, and murmuring to each other.

Sam caught a pungent phrase: "... the most exquisite person I've ever known..." and it was uttered in the throbbing voice of passion, the doctor's voice.

He checked himself, but they did not move when Sam passed. He wasn't interested in lovelorn doctors. He passed the twins' house, and the old turkey gobbler's. Anita Mendoza was standing in her doorway, a slender shadow made alluring by the purple dusk.

"Good evening, redhead."

"Hello, beautiful."

"How did you enjoy our Mr. Karlov?"

"Does anybody ever enjoy your Mr. Karlov?"

"He is a great man."

"I'll take your word for it."

"You rubbed him the wrong way."

"Yeah. I may rub his nose with four knuckles the right way—straight up."

"Stay here awhile, redhead, and you may change your opinions."

Sam lit a cigarette, then held up the match and let its light play on her face. Night had come. Miss Mendoza, with her half-lidded eyes, looked wicked and more sinister than ever. There was a crooked smile at her lips. Her bobbed black hair glistened.

"Tough," Sam said. "You're all plenty tough. I didn't need a set of diagrams."

"You asked for it."

"You've got a nice set-up," Sam drawled. "It looks airtight and bulletproof. But is it?"

"You say such mystifying things, Captain Shay," she drawled, imitating him.

"I'll bet you'll understand some of them before I've been here long, sweetheart," Sam replied, and strolled on.

At the end of the scattered row of houses, he turned and walked back. She was still standing in the doorway, smoking a cigarette.

"You carry it," Sam said, "in your left stocking."

"And I'm faster on the draw than you are, Captain Shay."

"Don't bet a little thing like your life on that." He paused and said deliberately: "As a matter of fact, I think I've got you all wrong. I don't think Ray Baxton is on this island."

"Really?"

"Yeah. I'm so sure of it that I'm going to tell my gang we're going to pull out. You see, we haven't got a scrap of real evidence to prove he's here. The tide will be running out about midnight, and I think we'll be running out with it."

Sam walked on. That hint ought to produce results reasonably soon. What he could not understand was this: if Ray Baxton was on Murder Island, if he was a prisoner of Karlov's, why was there this delay? Karlov had nothing to gain by waiting. If Ray Baxton was here, why was Karlov stalling at all?

Sam was sure that Ray Baxton was here and that Karlov was stalling. Why?

He intended giving the breadfruit tree a wide berth. The fat silver stars didn't show the lovers to him until he was almost upon them. They were still standing there, close together. Dr. Hobb was still talking in that throbbing voice, and the blue-haired girl stood in an attitude of entrancement, or so it seemed to Sam. It was weird. He suddenly thought of Sally Lavender, who was the only woman he had ever loved—the most beautiful and the crookedest woman in the Far East. She would pour knockout drops into his drink while she was whispering love words to him. In fact, she had. Even if Sally were respectable, he could never imagine himself talking to her as Dr. Hobb was talking to the blue-haired girl.

SAM STROLLED ON toward blackbeard's castle. He had thrown away his cigarette and he walked with the stealth of a panther. He sat down under a tree a hundred feet from the door and stared at the house and listened. The door was closed, and the barred gate was closed. He saw no lights and heard no sound.

He must have sat there an hour when a figure came

flitting through the trees and approached the barred gate. Without alarm or surprise, Sam appreciated that the figure was Koori—lovely, mysterious, innocent little Koori!

This was unexpected. He had been convinced the visitor would be the bobbed-haired woman, with her message.

Koori went to the gate and reached through the bars and thumped softly on the door. Presently the door opened. In the starlight, Sam could see the thin figure of a man in white. Cassius, the manservant.

Words were exchanged. The door closed. Koori slipped away and vanished toward the lagoon.

Sam got up and watched her disappear, then he went to the door but did not knock. He walked along the side of the house, passed the barred and darkened windows, and turned and went along the side of the house until he came to the hill. He picked his way among shrubbery and rocks until he was above the house. He walked softly across the roof to the other side and down the hill to the front of the house, taking his time, listening, peering in at every window he could reach. He saw nothing, heard nothing.

His inspection only proved his suspicions—that this house was as tight as a drum, that its contents were as mysterious and unknown as the contents of an unlabeled tin can.

The question remained as before: Was Ray Baxton here? Was he in this house or on this island? Sam suspected Karlov, but mightn't Karlov be, after all, nothing but a radical, a nut? So far, there had not been the slightest proof that Ray Baxton was on Murder Island—nothing but that chart which the man in the red sash—Chester Cave—had

Sam's hands clutched like an eagle's claws.

wanted to sell to Marthana for $50,000, and which Sam had obtained by force.

Something flew out of the dark with a faint fluttering and struck Sam a sharp tap on the side of the head. He dropped down quickly and looked about him, reaching for his holster; but he saw nothing moving and heard no sound but the distant booming of the surf on the barrier reef. After a moment, he struck a match and found what had struck him. It was a pebble wrapped in a piece of cloth. When he saw what the cloth was, he snatched it up and ran toward the house which he and the others were occupying.

He called: "Marthana!" as he went in the door. The house appeared to be deserted. A ship's lantern dimly lighted the

room which he shared with Rufe Pound and Willie Ru.
The *serang* was asleep on a cot.

Marthana's door opened and she came out.

"Where's Rosen?"

"I don't know."

"Look at this," he said. He showed her the cloth he had
picked up. It was a handkerchief. It was stained along one
edge with blood, dried black. In one corner the initials R
B were embroidered in dark blue.

Marthana cried: "Ray Baxton's handkerchief! Where'd
you find it?"

He told her the circumstances, then said: "Now, who
would have done that?"

She said breathlessly: "Ray Baxton is on this island!"

The hunchback came in and Marthana showed him
the handkerchief. He looked at it and panted: "It's Ray's!
Where'd you find this?"

Sam told him. Rosen said: "That settles it! Ray is on
this island!"

He was genuinely agitated, or he appeared to be. Sam
wondered where he had been. He wondered where Koori
was. He wondered who had thrown the pebble wrapped in
the handkerchief: Cassius or Koori? Or—who?

At all events, his hint to Anita Mendoza had been acted
upon speedily. Ray Baxton was somewhere on Murder
Island.

In low, tense voices they discussed plans. They talked for
an hour. It was finally decided to search the island carefully,
starting early in the morning. If Ray Baxton was not found,
nor any trace of him, they would then take steps toward
getting into and searching the fortress of Manuel Karlov.

"I'm convinced," Rosen said, "that he is being held in Karlov's house. But we must exhaust every possibility first."

He was trembling with eagerness. Marthana was big-eyed and rigid with excitement.

"Get to bed, both of you," Sam said finally. "Searching the island is going to be a tough chore. You'll need a good night's sleep."

RELUCTANTLY, THEY LEFT. Sam smoked a cigarette and went to bed. He heard Rufe Pound walking up and down, doing sentry duty. He heard Dr. Hobb come in. Much later—at least an hour later—he heard Koori come in. She had to pass the door of his room. She came stealthily along the hall, her sandals whispering on the coral floor. Of them all, she puzzled Sam the most. He knew that she was somehow involved in this mystery, yet he could not see how she fitted into any intrigue.

Considering possible ways of storming Karlov's fortress if the search of the island revealed nothing, he fell asleep—and was awakened shortly before dawn by Marthana. She was fully dressed. She held a burning candle in her hand, and he could see there were tears in her eyes.

She whispered: "Meet me on the beach, skipper. I've got to have a talk with you."

She went out. Sam slipped into sneakers, pants and sweater, and went down to the beach. Marthana was sitting on the palm trunk. There was some light in the sky, and it was increasing every instant—the swift upsurge of tropical dawn. A streak of silver-gray turned gold, then pink; the deep-blue of the night sky was shot with a suffusion of pearly color.

She looked up at him, and her eyes were still wet.

He said: "You're thinking about Jeff again."

Marthana did not deny it. But she said, "Well, it's Koori. What are you going to do about that child, Sam?"

"Do?"

"She's so in love with you!"

"Applesauce! She's a little, double-crossing—"

"Wait a minute, skipper! One thing at a time. She's in love with you. She's simply sick about it. She cries herself to sleep. She's losing weight. Why don't you talk to her? I agree that you're right. She's double-crossing us, and she's eating out her heart. I think she loves you so much that she'll come clean. I think she wants to make a clean breast of everything. That poor child is simply crazy about you, Sam. You can make her talk."

"How? By making love to her?"

"Of course."

"Nothing doing."

"She won't talk unless you do."

"She wouldn't talk if I did. You're wrong."

"Sam, listen to me. Maybe you've never been in love, but I'll bet, if you have, that you've never been in the state that poor girl is in. We both agree, don't we, that she smuggled herself away on this trip for a purpose, and that that purpose has something to do with Jeff's murder and Ray's kidnaping? In short, she knows something of vital importance that she intends to profit by."

"Yes."

"We can go further than that, Sam. We can guess that she knows there is very real, very great danger for some or all of us."

"How can we guess that?"

"By that look in her eyes! Terror, Sam—stark terror! And can you imagine how that girl, loving you, feels, torn as she is? Oh, she'll talk. Make love to her. Make ardent love to her."

"I couldn't do it."

"To save our lives?"

"No. Because I'd botch it."

"You mean, you'd hesitate—with our lives at stake?"

"Yes. Because I know the Oriental temperament."

"Koori isn't Oriental! She's as white as I am!"

"I don't know what Polynesians are. All I know is that they have the Oriental slant. She has a secret. It was put into her head by her old man. You could torture her to death and she wouldn't spill that secret. I could make love to her until I was hoarse—and she wouldn't talk."

"Let me send her here. Try it!"

"There's no use, sister. If there's anything to find out, let Hobb find it out from Faustine Fife."

Marthana shook her head. "I don't trust him any more than you do. I don't even know that he's sincere. That weird affair may simply be an elaborate device to keep Karlov informed of everything we say. It's up to you."

"All right," Sam said decisively. "Send her along."

"You'll make love to her?"

"I'll do my best."

"Your best has got to be good, Sam. Girls in love are very sensitive—very intuitive. You've got to make love to her as you've never made love in your life!"

"I'll do my best, sister."

"Wait here. I'll send her."

SAM WAITED. HE watched the sunrise. The island was

awakening. A faint breeze had sprung up, carrying to him the sweet mysterious fragrance of the island, of foliage still dew-drenched, of night flowers preparing to close with the rising sun. The sun rose behind a barrier of cumulous clouds and turned them suddenly from slate-gray to gold and red.

The voice of the island girl said: "You wanted me, captain."

In the golden diffusion of light from the clouds, she was as lovely as she was mysterious—young and fresh and unafraid. Her eyes, in her slim golden face, were dark and large. She was unsmiling.

"Sit down, Koori."

She did not obey at once. She was wearing a flowered blue *sarong* and a paler blue jacket and blue sandals. There was a star flower in her luxuriant black hair. Her personality, sometimes so charming, was withdrawn. He knew only that this slim girl was quite fearless. Yet her eyes looked frightened.

She sat down. He reached out and took her hand. It was warm, but it was trembling.

He said gently: "Koori, do you like me?"

Her long black lashes came up, then dropped. "You know I like you, Sam."

"You know why I came to Murder Island, too, don't you?"

"I—" she began, and stopped.

"You know that my best friend was cold-bloodedly murdered and thrown overboard from the Baxton yacht."

"Yes, I know"—a whisper.

"And you know why I've come here."

"To find the person who did it."

"Yeah. To find the person who did it. To find the person who did it and take his neck in my hands and snap it!"

"Yes," she whispered, but she did not meet his eyes.

"Another thing you know by this time is that we're in a dangerous spot. Something's wrong. You know that. If something wasn't wrong, there wouldn't be all this stalling."

"You mean—Ray Baxton may be dead?"

"I don't know, Koori. Maybe that. Maybe something else. I'm only sure of one thing: this man Karlov is very dangerous. He may be a madman, or he may not, but he's dangerous. So are the rest of this crew. Do you remember that fellow we found outside my room in Raffles?"

Koori nodded.

"That knife was put there by an expert."

The Princess of Saballa nodded again. "Yes, Sam."

"That's the kind of people we're dealing with. They'd slip a knife between your ribs—or mine—just as easy as that. Do you know what I'm getting at?"

"No, Sam."

"We've got to stick together. If this gang jumped you, I'd fight for you with my last breath. You know that, don't you?"

"Yes!"

"You know all this, and you say you like me—"

"I do like you!" Koori said passionately.

"Are you playing fair? That's what I want to know. It's what I've got a right to know."

She looked at him a moment and burst into tears. Sam quickly threw an arm about her shoulders and pulled her against him and hugged her. He said gruffly, "Come on, baby, snap out of that right away!"

She did not try to pull away, but she stopped crying.

She stared miserably at the sand and sniffled a little. The perfume in her lustrous black hair made Sam a little uneasy.

"Why were you crying?"

"I don't know," she said despairingly. And she was suddenly fierce. "How about that hunchback? Do you think he's to be trusted? Do you think he's playing square with you?"

"Why not?"

"He's too clever!"

"What's on your mind? Say it!"

"It's intuition."

Sam was suspicious, but he said: "You think he's in with Karlov? You think he framed up all this with Karlov? Is that what you think?"

"I don't know!" she wailed.

Koori's hands were in her lap. Sam covered them with one of his hands, gathered them into a small, warm bundle which he squeezed.

Her hands were limp in his hand. Her body against his was limp, yet he knew it would respond in an instant to him, that she would be in his arms loving him, kissing him, clinging to him if he said the right thing in the right way.

He said: "Koori, why were you crying?"

The island girl looked swiftly into his green eyes. Her eyes suddenly narrowed and became hard. He knew he had said the wrong thing in the wrong way. But it was beyond him to play this game as Marthana wanted him to play it. It called for a kind of hypocrisy that he didn't possess.

Koori freed her hands and stood up. Her small round breasts were moving up and down with her fierce breathing.

She said: "You're contemptible!" And she walked away.

24

JUNGLE DEATH

SAM RETURNED ANGRILY to the house. He was angry at himself for having tried to do a thing which he had loathed; he was angry at Koori for her refusal to meet him on his own terms of honesty and loyalty and friendship.

He watched Koori at breakfast. She hardly glanced at him. He watched Ben Rosen, too. Once when Sam caught him staring at him, the lawyer glanced quickly away. Dr. Hobb was preoccupied, too, hardly eating, looking dreamily off into space.

Sam announced that he intended to explore the island today, or as much of it as he could cover. He was a little surprised at the alacrity with which Dr. Hobb said that he would go. Sam glanced at Koori. Her lashes were down. They came up. Her eyes were dark and brooding.

"I hate walking in the jungle," she said.

The four of them—Sam, the lawyer, the doctor, and Marthana—started immediately after breakfast, taking their pistols, water and sandwiches, as they would be gone, Sam said, most of the day.

A path led out of the settlement and over the brow of the hill near Karlov's house. This path ended at the spring—the only fresh water spring on the island. Beyond was jungle.

And this was true jungle—tall trees with branches and foliage woven into a mat-like ceiling, with green light below, laced with vines. Nothing but great pale ferns grew on the floor of this strange, hushed, room-like space.

Sam found a faint trail and led his party through two miles of equatorial jungle. Beyond was a torn and tortured land of steep black hills and gorges, some running down to the sea, others paralleling it. In this region—all along this side of the coast—were the caves. There were dozens, hundreds of them, in the black lava of which the hills were composed, and here was a maze, too, of banyan trees, with their gnarled trunks.

After a pause for lunch, the party, of its own accord, broke into two halves. The lawyer and the doctor struck inland a little way, and Sam and Marthana began an exploration of the caves along the shore.

Shortly after midafternoon, the sky was overcast. Black clouds rolled up from the north. A squall passed close to the island, whipping the waves into a white fury. It was a tropical phenomenon. The miniature hurricane swept past within a half mile of the shore, but the island remained as still as death.

Sam and Marthana, on a hilltop, preparing to descend the hill, watched the squall sweep past and vanish in a churn of blackness to the south, and they commented on their common uneasiness.

And as they turned to go down, that sense of looming disaster was upheld by a sudden, strangling scream of terror.

It came from the valley where Ben Rosen and Dr. Hobb were supposed to be exploring caves.

When Sam and Marthana, scrambling up the other side of the gorge, reached the top, they saw nothing at first but the runneled black slopes of the gorge, then, south of them, they saw a figure coming toward them along the ridge of the opposite wall. It was Dr. Hobb.

Then Sam saw the crumpled white figure in the bottom of the gorge. He started down the hill. He saw that it was Ben Rosen. And when he was halfway down, he saw the blood. But it was the position of the head in relation to the body that chilled him and set the hair at the back of the scalp to bristling. The lawyer was lying flat on his stomach in the black sandy wash at the bottom of the gorge, but his face was straight up!

25

WHAT KIND OF MONSTER?

SAM CALLED TO Marthana: "You'd better not come any closer," but she came, quiet and pale as a ghost.

The hunchback had been killed in the same manner, by the same incredible creature that had, according to the islanders, killed Karlov's daughter, Anita Mendoza's brother, and Mace Littlejohn.

Ben Rosen had been strangled to death, but it was not an ordinary strangling. The killer had not only strangled him, but had crushed his neck to a bloody pulp, flesh and bones alike.

Gazing at that crushed neck, Sam was the victim for a moment of a wave of superstitious terror, for it was incredible to him that any living beast or brute or monster could have such strength in one hand as to break down human flesh and bones and sinew. Not even a python could crush flesh and bone so horribly, for Sam had seen corpses that had been strangled by these powerful snakes. There were the telltale finger marks and in the black wash all about the dead man Sam saw the marks of the fantastic beast at the tales of which he had scoffed so. Long, narrow marks, they were, with no toe or heel marks—as if the beast walked on singularly narrow feet which were little more than long bones.

The hunchback's eyes bulged dreadfully. And as Sam approached he detected the revolting smell which, the blue-haired woman and the others had declared, the beast always left hanging in the air. It was the smell of decaying flesh. It was like the breath of a tiger, and it sent new chills through Sam.

He bent down to examine the marks on the throat. Dr. Hobb came up, puffing and gasping. He gurgled: "Oh, good God!" over and over. He knelt down beside the dead man and rolled him over. He looked up at Sam with horrified pale eyes from a blanched face.

"Did you see it?"

"No. We were on the other side of the hill."

The doctor jumped up and looked around him wildly, with his hand on the butt of his automatic, but Sam had already looked, and he knew that the beast had taken itself away. The tracks in the narrow sandy wash went only a dozen feet, then vanished as if it had taken to wings.

Dr. Hobb cried: "Now, do you believe in it?"

"I don't know what to think," Sam answered.

"But it killed him! It got him!"

"I still don't know what it is."

"Good Lord, are you still skeptical?"

Sam said in a shaken voice: "I don't know what to think, doctor. I've lived in these countries for seven years, and this is outside my experience."

Dr. Hobb tried to get himself under control. Almost sobbing, he kneeled beside the dead man and examined the mutilated and mangled neck.

"Five marks—just like the other. Five fingers!"

Marthana said faintly: "Sam, isn't it some kind of gorilla?"

He shook his head. "No ape leaves tracks like these. They're more like bird tracks."

"Could a giant bird have done this?"

"No giant bird would swoop down and strike and then fly away. Birds don't work that way. We'd have seen a bird large enough to do this. It wasn't a bird."

THEY RETURNED TO the settlement, and Sam sent Rufe Pound and the *serang* around in a boat for the corpse. He had been in the settlement only a few minutes when Karlov sent for him. He did not need Karlov's imperious command for his presence to realize what a blow Ben Rosen's death was to the purpose for which they had come here.

Ben Rosen was the only authorized representative of the Baxton Corporation among them; he alone could have made arrangements for Ray Baxton's ransom.

Cassius, the living skeleton, met Sam at the barred gate and ushered him into the corridor. Anita Mendoza was just leaving. She paused and looked at Sam. Her black eyes looked wild. She was pale. Only a few minutes before, outside, Sam had told her and the others about Ben Rosen's violent death.

"I came right away and told him," she said in a voice that shook. "You're to go right in. He—" She did not finish the sentence but walked quickly out of the house.

Cassius ushered him into the great room. It was lighted only by two candles, one at either end of the desk. Karlov was pacing the floor, slowly beating his hands together. His blue eyes looked even more mad than they had yesterday. His curly black hair was rumpled. His skin was as white as wax.

When he saw Sam, he stopped in his pacing and snarled: "Is it true? Was Rosen killed?"

"Yes."

"How did it happen? Describe just how it happened!"

Sam described the tragedy. The man with the spade beard listened to him with arms held rigidly at sides, his blue eyes fixed fiercely on Sam's face.

He said, when Sam had finished: "What a tragedy! What a horrible tragedy!"

And Sam knew that he meant merely that it was tragic that the only man in the Far East who might have negotiated officially for Ray Baxton's release was dead.

The probable consequences were serious indeed. Karlov could have held Rosen as hostage for the delivery here, or at some distant place, of the ransom. Without Rosen, the whole kidnap scheme was a failure. More than that, the uncertainty of putting through a deal, the jeopardy in which Karlov was automatically placed, was a threat against Ray Baxton's life. For wasn't it likely that Karlov, seeing his scheme ruined, would secretly kill Ray Baxton and so destroy the only item of evidence against him?

Karlov curtly dismissed Sam, and there was nothing for Sam to do but go. Cassius, armed, had been standing just behind him all during this interview, and Karlov was in no mood for any kind of discussion.

Marthana was waiting for him in the dusk outside, a pale and worried girl. When he had told her about Karlov's frantic attitude, she saw what Sam had seen, and said:

"He'll kill Ray." And when Sam said nothing: "What are we going to do, skipper?"

"Find him," Sam said grimly.

"But these people won't let you near where he is!"

"I'll find him!" It was, Sam knew, his last, his only chance at tracking down the real murderer of Jeff Carmichael—to find Ray Baxton, and to get the story from Ray Baxton's lips.

26

SAM IS TRAPPED

RUFE POUND AND the serang returned with the body of
the hunchback. A grave was dug and Sam read the burial
service. It was a constrained and rather horrified gathering. The blue-haired girl clung to Dr. Hobb's arm and
wept softly. Anita Mendoza stood close to Sam and stared
at him from time to time with dry-eyed bitterness. Koori
stared at the grave, pale and wet-eyed.

Marthana did not weep. She was pale, and she looked
crushed. Sam understood what her thoughts must have
been. She had embarked on this errand sheerly through a
sense of duty. She felt she owed it to the man to whom she
was engaged but no longer loved, to represent him, to give
what aid she could to the task of establishing in a way that
would satisfy any court that Ray Baxton was either dead or
alive. In Ben Rosen's death, she saw complete frustration
to that plan. Anything might happen now, but whatever it
was would be horrible, she was sure.

Yet, even in her despair, she could not begin to evaluate
the sheer horror of the events to come.

No one had an appetite for supper. When it was over,
Sam took a pocket flashlight and with his automatic
strapped to his side, slipped through the darkness to black-

beard's castle. He had only one hope—to find Baxton before it was too late.

The large white coral house in the side of the hill was silent and dark. Not a glimmer of light showed at any window.

Sam went to the door of iron bars, reached through and tapped lightly on the thick wood inner door. After an interval, it was opened by the manservant.

Sam whispered. "Come here!"

And when the man came close enough, Sam reached swiftly through the bars and grabbed the skinny neck in hands that shot out like the clutching claws of an eagle.

He pulled the servant toward him, until Cassius's death's-head face was jammed between two of the bars. His eyes were bulging. He was struggling frantically. With the skinny neck held firmly in both hands, Sam pressed down on the man's Adam's apple with both thumbs.

So firmly did he hold the man's neck that in spite of his kicking legs and flailing arms, Cassius did not free himself, did not emit so much as a squeak of sound. His mouth flew open and he made hideous grimaces. His eyes bulged more and more, and suddenly he went limp.

Sam held him up with one hand. With the other he secured the key to the door. He unlocked it and slipped into the corridor.

With the pistol in his right hand, the flashlight in his left, he tiptoed down the corridor and into the large room where he had twice seen Karlov. The king of Murder Island was not in the room.

Bitterly disappointed, Sam returned to the corridor. If

he could have captured, overpowered Karlov, this game of wits would have been won.

Sam went down the corridor. There were no more doors on either side of it until he had gone more than fifty feet. As he had guessed, the house was built deep into the hill. **AT THIS DOOR** he stopped. It was a stout oak door. He tried the knob. It was locked. He went on another twenty-five feet and came to a stairway. At this stairway, the corridor came to a dead end.

He climbed the stairs cautiously, with his pistol ready. The stairs ended in another corridor, identical with the one downstairs except for the doors on either side—four to a side.

He stopped, listened, heard nothing. He called softly: "Baxton! Ray Baxton!"

He strained his ears for answering sounds until they roared, but there were no answering sounds. He tried the next door. It, too, was locked. He called again: "Baxton! Ray Baxton! Answer me!"

But there was no answer. With thumping heart, Sam tiptoed on down the corridor. At each door he stopped, tried the knob and, finding the door locked, softly called: "Baxton! Answer me!"

The last door that he tried was, perhaps, the one he was looking for. Of them all, the doorknob of this one was less rusty, and it had a rubbed look.

He called: "Baxton! Ray Baxton! Answer me!"

Sam placed his ear to the panel and listened. He distinctly heard someone stirring about on the other side!

A light flashed on behind him and a deep, nasal voice

said: "Don't shoot, Cassius. Were you looking for someone, captain? Can I assist you?"

Sam spun about, but he did not raise the pistol. Cassius, magically restored, was standing beside Karlov with his feet apart, a rifle at his shoulder, aimed, and no doubt ready to fire.

Karlov held the light. He was apparently unarmed.

Sam glared at him, but repressed his fury at the interruption and drawled, "What do you think, Mr. Karlov?"

"All my facilities are at your disposal, Captain Shay."

"Okay. Open this door."

"I regret, captain, that there is no key to that door. To the other doors—yes."

"So Ray Baxton is behind this door."

"Is he? Are you so sure?"

Sam banged on the door and shouted: "Ray! Answer me!"

Again he heard sounds as of someone moving about.

Karlov had his head tilted, as if he, too, were listening for an answer. He said: "You see, captain? You guessed wrong."

"He's here."

"All right, captain. Supposing we grant that? Supposing we admit that Ray Baxton is here. What then?"

"Good," Sam said briskly. "Now we're getting somewhere. Let's stop all this hocus-pocus and talk like business men. You're holding Baxton for ransom. And I could block your game."

The black-bearded man smiled. "Could you, captain? How?"

"By sending that ship away and having an American gunboat here within four days!"

"And in those four days, what would happen to Mr. Baxton?"

"That's better," Sam said. "That's much better. If you'd only done this yesterday, Ben Rosen wouldn't be dead now. You're not a fool. What are you waiting for?"

The black-bearded man looked at him amusedly. "Are you sure I am waiting, Captain Shay? Are you sure that you aren't placing an exorbitant value on my time? Time is nothing but a yardstick used by stupid people to gage their futile little endeavors. Perhaps, Captain Shay, we need a little more time to cool off."

He smiled.

"Okay!" Sam snapped. "You win! State your figure. How much do you want? I'll do what you say. I'll bring the money here or wherever you say, conditional, of course, on absolute proof that Ray Baxton is alive. What's the figure?"

The king of Murder Island shook his head. "Can you find your way out, unassisted?" he said coldly.

Sam stared at him a moment in incredulity. He glanced at the man with the rifle. Sam couldn't shoot first—or he mightn't shoot first. The risk was too great.

He dropped the automatic into his holster and strode past them. His back tingled as he went, but the human skeleton didn't shoot.

27

SAM MEETS THE MONSTER

THERE WAS NOTHING Sam could do now but settle down to an attitude of watchful waiting. He was puzzled and furious. He could see no reason for Karlov's evasiveness, if Ray Baxton was there and alive. Why had he avoided talking terms with Ben Rosen at that first meeting? Why had he refused to talk terms tonight? It was baffling, and it led Sam to fantastic suppositions, one of which was so fantastic that he refused to credit it—and later sorely wished that he had.

Returning to the house he shared with Marthana, Koori and Dr. Hobb, he found that Koori had slipped out on some mysterious errand. Dr. Hobb had gone out without explanation or apology and met the blue-haired girl at their trysting place under the breadfruit tree. That, too, was mystifying.

And that night, the second of their sojourn on Murder Island, the beast returned to the settlement. Sam was aware of a disturbing odor once during the night—the odor of corrupt flesh—but he did not wake up fully. By dawn, the beast had come, done its work and gone.

It had dug up the corpse of Mace Littlejohn, stripped the bones clean of the decaying flesh—and gone again. It had taken everything but the left leg bone, and that was stripped almost clean. It looked as if it had been gnawed.

It was sickening. It was far worse than death. It plunged the little settlement into a state of morbid despair. Even Sam, inured to violence and violent death, was sickened.

He had forgotten that this horrible creature, whatever its nature might be, was reputed to return on the night following burial and devour its victim. And it occurred to him, as suddenly, that tonight would be the night following Ben Rosen's funeral!

He decided to stand guard all night over the lawyer's grave. He mentioned his plan to no one, not even the two sentries, Rufe and Willie Ru. But he told them: "If you hear me yell, come. But don't come under any other conditions. Stay on the job. I'm beginning to have some new suspicions, and I want this house watched. If Hobb tries to slip out later than eleven o'clock, stop him. He is not to leave this house any later than that."

Armed with his automatic, Sam went through the grove to the clearing, to the spot where Ben Rosen was buried. The grave was about twenty feet from the gutted grave of Mace Littlejohn. Near it was a large hibiscus bush in flower.

Settling down near this, so that he could not be seen from the grave, Sam prepared to pass the night. The settlement became quiet. One by one the lights went out. A faint breeze stirred the fronds of the coconut palms and set up their soft, somehow sad murmur as of rain gently falling. Bats flew about. Night birds chirped and, from the jungle, came the strident hum of insects. The mosquitoes were thick, and if there had been any likelihood of Sam's falling asleep, these stinging vicious insects prevented it.

The night became quieter. The breeze died down. The booming of the surf on the barrier reef came as a low lulling murmur. Now and then, Sam heard the distant thump of a footstep as Rufe Pound or the *serang* reached the end of his beat and turned.

A tall shadow darker than the night crept silently through the palms toward the clearing in which Sam sat, alert and waiting, with his automatic on one knee. The time was about three o'clock.

In utter silence, the tall shadow moved closer and closer to the hibiscus bush. The red-headed man's first knowledge of its approach was the sudden pressure of prickly fingers about his throat. The unknown killer had not pounced. It had simply reached out from the darkness, and it had him now by the throat!

In his horror at that obscene touch, he forgot his pistol. He dropped it and reached up swiftly with both hands. His hands closed on prickly fur, on a wrist as strong as steel, as rigid as rock.

His breath was bottled in his lungs. He tried to force it out in a yell, but only a little breath could be forced past that closing, relentless grip. It came as a faint hissing. With all his strength, he tried to pluck that clenching hand away from his throat. The stars above him wheeled and spun. Blackness in his brain threatened to shut off even that whirling, dim impression. His chest muscles labored to force air out and in, but the hand with its prickly fur had closed too far.

He was, it was evident, about to meet the fate of those

others. He struggled. He kicked, he clawed, and as he did so, his struggles grew weaker and weaker. He felt his eyes bulging. His mouth writhed and gasped for air, but it could have no air. His windpipe was stopped. He was choking. And suddenly the blackness in his brain overwhelmed him.

28

MADNESS

JUST WHAT TOOK place from the moment when he lost consciousness in the grip of that hideous hand to his full awakening, Sam could never be quite sure. When he was fully conscious, the sky was gray with dawn, and the grave of Ben Rosen was empty.

There had been an interlude of at least two hours which were highly mystifying. Sam was certain that he had been almost conscious any number of times in that period. It was inconceivable that he had remained unconscious for such a long period from that brief strangling. There were many marks on his neck. He concluded that the beast had leisurely gone about its feast and had, from time to time, when Sam was at the verge of recovering consciousness, throttled him again and again.

Why this obscene monster had not killed him remained a baffling mystery.

It had scooped the sand out of Ben Rosen's grave, and it had evidently devoured the body. Nothing but the two arm bones were left behind, stripped of all flesh. When Sam returned to awareness that dawn, he saw these naked bones gleaming in the faint oncoming light.

He was too ill, too weak to move or to cry out for some

time. His neck was so sore, so tender that he could not touch it without wincing and groaning. He fell back and lay, looking up at the sky, taking in deep lungfuls of the cool night air, putting down the revolt in his stomach at what his eyes had seen.

When he could sit up again, he groaned, and it was this groan that brought Rufe running. He helped Sam to his feet and brushed the sand off his clothes and babbled questions. The big mate was almost fainting from sheer terror.

The hysteria in his voice aroused the others, and in a little time the entire colony came running, in ones and twos, to the clearing.

It was the first any of them had known of Sam's dangerous plan, and of them all, it seemed to Sam, Koori was the most terrified, the most distressed. She had not paused long enough to slip into a dressing gown. In a pair of Marthana's borrowed pajamas, she came running through the palms, her black hair streaming out behind. She was sobbing as she ran.

She sped straight to Sam with her arms outflung. She threw her arms about him, pinning his arms to his sides, and holding him with a fierceness and strength that he recalled later with some astonishment. She held him for a moment, sobbing all the time, and when she let him go, she flung the hair back out of her face and stared up at him, still holding him fiercely, but this time only by the front of his shirt, fiercely holding handfuls of it.

She said huskily, in a strange, breathless voice: "What did you do this for, Sam? What did you do this for?"

He was so astonished at her emotion that he stammered: "Wh-why. I'm all right, baby."

She was staring at his bruised and swollen neck. "You should not have come here alone! You might have been killed!"

Marthana said tremulously, "It was foolish of you, skipper. Why you weren't killed is a mystery."

Koori said imperiously: "Come to the house. I will put something on that neck." Then she grew angry. "You are a fool! You are a great fool!" And she began sobbing again.

BACK IN THE house, she applied some kind of lotion to the bruises on Sam's neck, and it relieved the pain, but his throat remained so sore that he could hardly swallow.

Koori was evidently trying hard to keep herself under control, but she trembled all over, she made strange little grimaces and her eyes, in spite of her efforts, continually filled with tears.

"You should not have gone there!" she stormed.

"Why?"

"You should have known better!"

"What should I have known?"

"That it would kill you!"

"Sure! But what do you know that I don't know? Are we all going to be killed by this thing, one by one?"

She stared up at him. Her very eyes seemed to flutter. She cried: "How can I say?"

"You could if you would. You could say plenty."

She was hovering close to him. He wasn't as angry as he sounded. He was more baffled and annoyed by her persistent mystery. It might have turned to anger in an instant if it had not been for the girl's very solicitude, her tenderness and her undeniable loveliness. Her anxiety over him made her more appealing to Sam than she had ever been in the past. He could have pulled her down on his knees at that moment. Something close to love for this slim, golden-skinned girl was stirring in the red-headed man at that moment, but the emotion was washed away on a sudden wave of anger. If she knew something that he should know, why didn't she talk?

The next moment, Cassius walked into the room and said, in his croaking voice: "Manuel Karlov wishes to see you at once. But you are to go unarmed."

"Why?"

"Those are his orders."

Sam took his automatic from the holster and tossed it on the bed. "All right. What difference does it make?"

He accompanied Cassius to the house and into the large gloomy room. Karlov wore a purple dressing gown, and he was again pacing the room.

When Sam came into the room, the black-bearded man snatched up a candle, and held it close to Sam's chest. He stared at the red-headed man's neck and said with passion: "You utter damned fool! How did you let this happen?"

Sam glared into the piercing blue eyes and said angrily: "What do you know about it?"

"If you fool with that thing, you'll get killed. I know— and you ought to know. Keep away from it!"

"What is it?" Sam barked. "Your pet gorilla?"

Karlov's breath hissed through his almost closed lips. His eyes, Sam thought, were utterly insane. "I've warned you, captain. You were lucky. You don't realize how lucky you were to escape with only those bruises. It kills!" His voice had risen almost to a shriek. "It kills! It doesn't let its victims escape!"

In spite of himself, Sam burst out: "What is it? What is it?"

"I don't know," Karlov answered, in a voice suddenly spent and lifeless. "Go after it, why don't you? Hunt it down!"

Sam had already decided on that course. Karlov's madness was contagious. Leaving the house, Sam was for a moment under the impression that the very air of this island bred madness, or the compulsion to madness, as if it came to the brain in a vapor breathed off by the very spirit of Murder Island.

WITH NO STOMACH for breakfast, Sam organized the hunt. Armed with rifles, he, Dr. Hobb, Rufe Pound and the *serang* set forth through the jungles. The strange footprints of the killer vanished as they had before—just beyond the spring. Past this point was grass and undergrowth too thick for them to be seen, but at a point near the jungle one of the long, strange tracks was found.

They spent the day in the jungle and in the thick bushland to the west of it. They found no more tracks. They found no further evidence that the thing, whatever it was, existed.

It was a day of nightmare and strange illusions.

Exhausted, the four men returned to the settlement that evening to report failure. At the house, Sam learned that Koori had eaten nothing all day, had had hysterics several times, and Marthana was in little better shape. It was evident that the morale of the group was on the verge of cracking.

After a spiritless supper, which Koori did not attend and

which no one else did more than touch, Dr. Hobb dressed, as usual, to keep his rendezvous with Faustine Fife.

Marthana said: "I think you ought to stay here tonight, doctor. There's too much in the air. I have the feeling that anything might happen."

Dr. Hobb said, with an irritable air, "I can't help it. I'm going."

Sam said, "She's right, doc. You'd better stick around."

Koori came to the doorway. She was as pale as death. Her eyes were enormous, and the dark circles under them made her look ill.

She said huskily: "Doctor, you're not going out."

He wheeled toward her angrily. He clenched his fists. He looked wildly at Sam and Marthana and cried: "You don't understand! I'm in love with her! I can't help it! I've decided to stay here!"

They stared at him. "You're nuts," Sam muttered. "There's something about this place that's driving us all nuts. Keep the lid on, doc. Keep away from that woman."

"I can't."

"Oh, you can't?"

"For God's sake, skipper," Marthana groaned, "let's not have a row!"

The handsome doctor was glaring at Sam. "What do you know about love? How about that lovely child there who's simply throwing herself at you? You aren't human!"

Sam said quietly: "That has nothing to do with this blue-haired gal. She's poison."

"If you say another word against her—"

"Wait a minute, doc. Take it easy."

Marthana, disregarding her own counsel, said warmly:

"The skipper's right, doctor. That woman isn't human. She's like those big sickly sweet pale flowers we saw growing in the jungle. She's too beautiful. She's deadly. She's like opium."

Dr. Hobb was white with rage. "Stop it!" he panted. "I won't listen to a word against her. I know all about her. She's told me! She's been Karlov's mistress. She's been the mistress of a dozen other men. Do you think that makes any difference?"

"No," Sam said, "but that isn't the point. We're in danger. We've got to stick together."

The handsome doctor looked wildly at him, at Marthana, at Koori, looking in the doorway, as if she were about to faint. He rushed out.

They heard him stumbling through the night toward that strange trysting place, the breadfruit tree.

Sam's jaw hardened. "Marthana," he said, "I'm afraid there's only one answer. We've got to get that fellow out of here. That woman isn't human. He's making love to a woman in the moon. Things are cracking up under us."

"Yes," Koori said faintly in the doorway, but there was such vehemence in her voice that Sam and Marthana both stared at her with alarm.

Sam walked over to her. "Yes?" he said quietly.

"Yes! Can't you feel it in the air?"

He whispered: "What, baby, what?"

"Death! Nothing but death!"

"Whose?"

"All of us! Every one of us!"

Marthana cried out: "Oh, Koori; stop being so damned

mysterious! Talk to us! Tell us what you know! We've been your friends. We're loyal friends."

Koori stared at her a moment, then bit her lip and with a little sob ran into her room and slammed the door.

Sam and Marthana turned and looked at each other.

She said wearily, "Skipper, I hate to admit it, but I feel licked."

And at that instant came the awful scream. It seemed to come from everywhere, from the air all about them, from the very ground on which they stood—a throbbing, gurgling sound of hideous implication.

Sam started for the door, but the blond girl was too fast for him. She ran to it and blocked his way and cried: "Don't you dare! If it's Hobb, he asked for it! Don't you risk yourself!"

He pushed her aside. As he did, the scream was repeated, but this time on a higher, thinner note. It sent chills into his bones and the hair at the nape of his neck bristled. There was—he could define it in no other way—blood in that scream.

He ran through the darkness. Halfway to the breadfruit tree, he detected the stench of rotting flesh. It filled him with a strange kind of mania. He could hardly breathe. His breath caught in his bruised throat. And he had again the sense that madness was distilled from the very essence of this place.

His flashlight picked them out when he was fifty feet away. They were lying near each other, the doctor and the blue-haired girl. Both were dead. Both had died instantly. The throat of each had been clutched and crushed by the prickly paw that had held Sam Shay unconscious for hours during the night.

29

ONE MORE DIES

SAM HEARD BEHIND him the sudden hysterical voice of Marthana. He did not pause. He shouted: "Go back and wait!" and ran on toward blackbeard's castle. The doors were closed. When he banged on the bars, Cassius opened the wooden door and slammed it shut again.

His muffled voice came through: "Drop that gun! Leave it in the sand!"

Sam was unaware that the automatic was still clutched in his hand. He dropped it to the sand and panted: "All right! Open up!"

The heavy inner door opened tentatively. The living skeleton unlocked the barred door and stepped cautiously back with a revolver or pistol ready in his hand.

Karlov was in his study, backed against his desk, both hands covering his face. He looked shrunken and ill.

Sam shouted: "Karlov!" and the king of Murder Island dropped his hands and stared at him.

"I know," he muttered. "It got her."

"It got them both!" Sam shouted.

"Both? The doctor too?"

"Yes, the doctor too!" Sam tried to control his voice, to put down the jittering of his nerves. Of the two of them, he was certain he was closer to madness than Karlov could possibly be.

"Look here, Karlov; we've got to do something drastic. We've got to clear out."

"Then clear out! Am I detaining you?"

"With Ray Baxton!"

"I will not talk about that tonight, captain."

Sam said furiously: "Why not? Why are you stalling? You're not fooling anybody. I know Ray Baxton is upstairs in that front room!"

Karlov panted: "Watch him, Cassius! Don't hesitate to shoot!"

Sam lost his patience entirely. He said savagely: "Stop acting like a damn fool! I'm not threatening you. We know you've got Baxton. Why won't you talk business? How much do you want? Name your price. Let's get this over with. Don't you want to leave here as badly as we do?"

"God, yes!" Karlov groaned.

"Then let's make a dicker and go."

"You don't understand, captain." For a moment the piercing blue eyes were almost imploring. It was as if, for that moment, he was on the verge of betraying a closely-guarded secret. "I can't go!"

"Why not?"

"I cannot leave this cursed place until my destiny is fulfilled."

Sam stared at him, for a moment speechless, actually gasping for breath. It was almost as if he had expected Manuel Karlov to say just that. It was in the air as definitely as the stench of rotting flesh had been in the air under the breadfruit tree a few minutes ago.

He did not know his own voice when it came: "Say what you mean, Karlov!"

But the king of Murder Island had recovered, was again in control of himself. He said coldly: "If you are afraid, Captain Shay, you can leave this island. No one is stopping you."

Sam would have sprung on him, in this sudden burst of murderous fury that swept over him, but Cassius was just behind him, his skinny finger curled about the trigger of the automatic pistol in his hand.

Sam ran out of the room and out of the house. He ran through the palms all the way to the other house. But as he neared it, he slowed to a walk and tried to compose himself. His pulses raced. His lungs felt hot. His hands were icy, damp. In his seven years of adventure in the Far East, in the islands of the southern seas, he had had many moments of terror and despair, but nothing to compare with this. He was at the end of his rope. He was as desperate as any drowning man.

He tried to calm himself, to be prepared for the ordeal of talking to the two girls.

MARTHANA WAS WAITING in his room, a small lump of frightened girl in a chair, bravely smoking a cigarette, fiercely puffing out the smoke.

She wailed: "Sam!"

"I saw Karlov. He's as crazy as a bat, but he's sane compared to me. Where's that girl?"

Koori answered: "Do you want me?"

"Come here!" he snapped.

She came into the room, walking like an automatom, her eyes enormous, her face a sickly green in the lantern light.

"I heard," she said.

He sucked in his breath, whistling. "Yeah, you heard. Both of them, strangled to death under that tree. Go on and talk!"

The Princess of Saballa dropped into a chair. She said, in a husky whisper: "What can I say?"

"What do you know about this? What do you know about any of this?"

She stared at him and her chin trembled. She dropped her face into her hand and her shoulders began to tremble.

Marthana groaned: "Oh, Sam, for Heaven's sake be kind to the kid. Koori, aren't you going to talk?"

The island girl's muffled voice said: "There's nothing I can say."

Sam began to pace the floor. He said: "Listen, Marthana; we've got to make a decision. I can't tell you how I feel about all this. It's something in my bones. There's something going on here as plain as the nose on my face, but I don't get it. I hate to admit I'm licked, but there can't be any more killings."

Koori lifted her face, wet with tears, and said in a choked voice: "Go! Both of you!"

He stared at her. "You know a lot, don't you?"

She said steadily: "You are fools not to go."

"Is that all you're going to say?"

"Isn't it enough?"

Sam and Marthana exchanged glances. He said: "I'll stay here. You go with Rufe and Willie to Batu Latu and bring back a Dutch gunboat. We'll call his bluff."

"No," Marthana said stubbornly. "Once we leave this

island, Ray is lost. We'll never see him dead or alive. You'll lose your chance of fixing the blame for Jeff's murder.

"We've gone through too much to back down now."

"It won't be backing down. I'm staying."

Marthana shook her head, "I'm sticking too. I'll see it through."

Koori said wildly: "No, no! Sam's right, Marthana. You go."

"Why?" Sam snapped. "Is her number up next?"

"She is sure to be killed if she stays!"

"How do you know?"

"I feel it! I know it!"

Sam advanced toward her, grimly. "Did Karlov tell you?"

She cried desperately: "Oh, no, no!"

The red-headed man looked menacing. "You knew Rosen was going to be killed! You knew Hobb was going to be killed! Is Marthana next?"

"She will be killed if she stays!" said Koori.

"Did Karlov," Sam said grimly, "tell you Rosen and Hobb were to be killed?"

"I'm warning Marthana now!" Koori wailed. "Won't you take her away from this dreadful place?"

"I'm not afraid of his killer," Marthana said quietly. "Koori, aren't you going to talk?"

"There's nothing more I can say."

"You admit you've been seeing Karlov!"

Koori sprang up. She was no longer crying. She said fiercely: "I won't be cross-questioned any longer!"

Sam reached for her wrists, but she eluded him; slipped past him to the door. She paused at the threshold in an attitude of one about to take flight. She looked at them pathetically.

She said in a strange voice: "Marthana, I love you. Sam, I love you too. I can say it now. You are the only man I ever loved. The only time I ever hated you was when you pretended to love me, to make me talk. Even if I were dying next minute, I couldn't talk. Haven't you lived in these countries long enough to realize that? You're deliberately being stupid."

Marthana said wearily: "What does she mean, Sam?"

He didn't answer. He started impetuously toward the girl in the doorway.

Koori cried: "Don't come near me!"

"But I love you," Sam said in a desperate voice.

She stared at him, as shocked as if he had slapped her. She shook her head. "No. You never could."

"I do. I mean it."

"I'm not your race."

"I'm telling you! And now you're afraid!"

"You're lying!"

Marthana cried. "Look at him! He isn't lying, Koori!"

"To make me talk!" Koori said huskily. "Just to make me talk! You haven't room for a woman in your life. Not me. Not any woman."

"What good," Sam said harshly, "would it do to talk now? You've said all there is to say."

"I can't. You're being cruel."

SAM WALKED TOWARD her, trying to hold her eyes. She made a little moaning sound. He intended to take her in his arms and assure her that he wasn't lying. He was suddenly certain that he loved her and that if he did not

instantly make her realize it, she would somehow escape
him forever. It might have been the madness of the night.
He didn't know. But he believed he was sure.

One of her hands was reaching up, in a tightly clenched
fist, along the doorjamb, as she turned and watched, not
his eyes, but his advancing feet. He saw, clasped within it,
a scrap of paper. But he did not think about it until later.

"Grab her!" Marthana shrieked.

But Koori was gone. Her hand containing the scrap of
paper flashed down, and she was out the doorway; running
into the darkness.

"Get her!" Marthana screamed.

Sam shouted: "Rufe! Stop her! Grab her!"

It was as if all the desperation bred by the night's events
was centered in the fleeing girl.

He heard a thump as Koori collided with Rufe, and
the mate's grunt, then, "Come back here!" He reported a
second later: "She got away from me, Skipper! She wiggled
away like a greased snake."

Off to the left, in the darkness, Sam heard the crackling
of a dead frond underfoot. He ran in that direction. And
when Koori eluded him, he went to Karlov's house and
waited. He was certain she would come here. She must
not come here!

He waited and listened, making himself small in the
denser blackness of a seagrape tree. His eyes grew used to
the starlight. The house was dark and silent as a tomb. And
Koori did not come.

He circled back toward the other houses. Anita Mendoza
and Hiram Fillow were having an argument in the house
occupied by the Slingrose twins. Their voices rose and fell.

"One cry out of you and I'll kill you!"

He might have learned much by eavesdropping, but he was more interested in finding Koori.

The air about him was faintly tainted with the smell of decomposing flesh. It made his flesh creep, and his hair bristle, and it accentuated the sharp small pulse at the back of his head.

He circled back to the beach, walking as stealthily, as warily as if death were stalking him.

Above the angry droning of the old turkey gobbler's voice, the voice of Anita Mendoza rose sharply in a shriek of rage. "I won't tolerate any more of it! It's gone too far! I won't!"

Her voice was muffled as suddenly as if a hand had been clapped over her mouth.

Back in the direction of blackbeard's castle, Sam heard a faint scuffling, as if some creature, some small animal, had been pounced upon and was being held, in its death struggles, by a larger.

His heart raced faster. His breath burned in his bruised throat. His eyes seemed to him to bulge out of his head as he stared in that direction. He heard a soft, faint thump; he cried out in a voice of awful despair: "Koori! Koori! Where are you?"

When there was no answer, he started at a run toward the sounds.

He found her lying, a small, crumpled, lifeless thing, not twenty feet from where the doctor and the blue-haired woman were lying.

30

KARLOV'S OFFER

SINGAPORE SAMMY DID not pause, but ran on. He took out his flashlight and sent the beam in a sweeping semi-circle. It picked out, near the top of the hill, a large, tall creature, black as the night from which it came, that might have been a giant bat. It seemed to have flapping wings that helped it as it scurried up the hill. It looked enormously tall and it seemed actually to float along over the hill.

There was not time for a shot. And halfway up the hill, Sam stopped. His heart was fighting for oxygen. The batlike killer was travelling too fast for him to hope to overtake it.

He returned to the murdered girl.

Alternate waves of illness and fury went through the red-headed man until he was trembling so he could hardly stand. He stood looking down at the dead girl and shook. Every muscle in his body joined in this palsy of hatred.

He flashed on his electric pocket light, but he did not send the beam into her face or on her neck. He knew what he would see, and he could not tolerate it. He knew that life had been crushed from her as it had been from all the others. And his despair, his helplessness filled him with a desperation so great that he could have sobbed.

Her hands were lying limp beside her. And he saw the scrap of paper which he had previously glimpsed when she stood in the doorway an instant before she ran to meet this dreadful fate.

The palm was upturned, with the fingers gently curling about the crumpled scrap of paper. As he picked it up, Rufe came pounding up, panting, flashing his light here and there, gasping questions as he came. Marthana was just behind the mate, with her own light, and other lights danced like witch-lights among the palms. Anita Mendoza came running fleetly, and strung out behind her were the Ringrose twins and the old man.

All had lights. All turned these white beams on the girl lying dead in the sand.

Sam did not look again. He could not look.

Rufe was muttering curses under his breath.

The bobbed-haired woman suddenly screamed: "I can't stand it! I can't stand any more of it!" She turned and ran, her voice still trailing out behind her, as thin, as high as the wail of the fabulous banshee. Hiram Fillow, muttering angrily, followed her.

Marthana fainted. The nickeled light slipped from her hand and dropped. She slid to her knees and fell over on the sand on her side.

It at least gave Sam something to do. He picked her up in his arms, recovered her electric torch, and carried her back to the house.

He arranged her on his bed, propped her feet up, and poured brandy into her mouth from the bottle. When she gagged and gasped, he rubbed her hands, slapped her cheeks and massaged the back of her neck.

While she fought her way back to consciousness, he drained the brandy bottle. He tossed the bottle into a corner.

Marthana's eyes were open. She was staring at him. She said, "Did you see it happen, skipper?" in a voice so feeble that he suspected all the fight was knocked out of her.

"No. But I saw it getting away."

She seized his arm and pulled herself up. She swung her legs over the side of the bed and sat beside him, her head resting heavily on his shoulder, her breath coming and going in little gasps.

"It looked like a bat. It looked nine feet tall. It was running up the hill too fast for a shot. I found this."

He had pushed the scrap of paper into his pocket. He pulled it out. It was only a shred of paper on which was written in Koori's round, childish handwriting, in pencil:

"Sam: A cat's claw is as swift as the swiftest steed."

Marthana read it. "What does it mean?"

"It's an old Javanese proverb. It means—a lot of things. A thing that doesn't seem important can be just as tremendous as something that seems important. That's the idea. But what does it mean now?"

"Does she mean we've been overlooking something that seems trivial?" Marthana's mouth quivered.

"Oh, Sam, she knew she was going to be killed."

"Yes," he groaned. He was desperately trying to reason out the meaning of that cryptic sentence. The hand of the batlike creature that crushed its victims' necks was like a claw—but what did the rest mean?

MARTHANA SAID, IN that crushed voice: "I think it's horrible. Why, why wouldn't she tell us?"

And Sam answered drearily: "Because we're east of the hundred and eightieth meridian, sister. They bring them up that way in this part of the world."

"But she was so crazy about you, Sam!"

"That doesn't cut any ice in these countries. We'll never know the truth, but we can come close to it. She couldn't speak, but she did her best to tip us off without speaking. Her old man—that foxy little sultan—sent her on this trip for a certain purpose. Money. Blackmail. It's what I said before—you could have tortured her to death and she wouldn't have talked. It's the way she was brought up. She wanted to talk, but she couldn't. This is as far as she could go. If we're smart, it means plenty. But it doesn't mean anything unless—"

"The claw means the claw of that thing!" Marthana cried.

"Oh, sure. But what does the rest of it mean? What does she mean by 'the steed'? What steed? A steed is a horse. If I had to swear on my life, I'd say it was a bat nine feet tall—a gigantic black bat!"

"Bats don't grow so large!"

"Not any bat I ever saw."

Marthana began to shiver. "Sam, you've got to puzzle this out. I can't. My brain is empty. It's nothing but fire and ice. I can't think of anything but that poor little thing lying—" Marthana began to cry. With her head on Sam's shoulder, without covering her eyes, she sobbed.

Sam didn't try to stop her. At length, she stopped of her own accord. She stared across the room at the ship's clock which Rufe had brought ashore from the chart-room. It was almost four o'clock.

The girl said fiercely: "Oh, it's so damnably unfair! That poor little thing—"

"Yeah," Sam took her up in a dry voice; "it's all unfair. Money! Eight hundred million bucks! Jeff killed—the best guy that ever lived, stabbed in the back and chucked overboard—all these other people killed. What for? The dough! Eight hundred million bucks! It's screwy. And what happens to you?"

"I don't care what happens to me!"

"Sure, you too! You fall in love with a great guy, and he gets a knife in the back. Why? Because some guy worth eight hundred million bucks is roaming around the South Seas. How many people are dead to date, all because of this one guy? Chester Cave, Bruno Reddy, Ben Rosen, Dr. Hobb, Faustine Fife, Koori and Jeff. That's seven. And how do we know Ray Baxton is still alive? Roll those bones, luck!"

"Stop!" Marthana wailed. "I can't stand it."

"Well, you've stood plenty. You've stood too much. We're checking out of here when that sun comes up."

"No," Marthana said, suddenly firm. "We're going to stick it out, skipper."

Dim grayness appeared at the windows. Dawn was coming.

Sam studied the scrap of paper with furrowed brows. A cat's claw is as swift as the swiftest steed.

RUFE POUND CAME into the room. He seemed to bristle all over. His face was angrily flushed. His small, piglike eyes were bloodshot.

"The livin' skeleton wants to talk to Miss Bondy. He wants to come in. Do I let him in?"

"Yes."

Rufe went to the door and growled: "All right. Come in, you."

Cassius came in. He wore a pistol belt. From one skinny flank dangled a holster with the butt of an automatic pistol showing. His sunken eyes had an unholy glow in them.

He said, in his croaking voice: "Where is the *serang?*"

Rufe answered: "He's aboard the schooner and what the hell business is it of yours?"

"Pipe down," Sam said. "Why is Willie aboard?"

"He's too scairt. He was scairt plenty by what happened to Mr. Rosen. When he heard Dr. Hobb yell that way, he scrammed. He couldn't take any more of it."

Sam said to Cassius: "What do you want?"

Karlov's manservant answered: "I have a message for Miss Bondy from Manuel Karlov. If she will assure him that there will be no prosecution, no attempt of any kind at retaliation, he will release Mr. Baxton."

"No money?" Sam snapped.

"No money. He is almost in a state of collapse as a result of all these killings. He is a sick man. He wants to leave this place as soon as possible. He is afraid he will be killed next. He is afraid that this monster has gone berserk and may rip the bars off the door and force its way in and get him. I have tried to reason with him, but—"

"*You* have tried—" Sam began, and entertained for a moment the fantastic thought that this creature, this living skeleton, was the master mind behind it all.

"Yes, I have tried. But he is in a state of terror."

"Tell him," Marthana said promptly, "that we accept his terms, but that Ray Baxton must be brought here at once."

The living skeleton shook his head. "Manuel Karlov insists that you go to his house at once and talk to him, assure him yourself."

"All right," Sam snapped, "we'll go."

"Not you, captain," Cassius said. "Only Miss Bondy."

"And the answer to that," Sam said, "is nuts."

"I'll go," Marthana said grimly.

"You'll not go," Sam said, as grimly. "It's a trick. It's a trap. You know what Koori said. Marthana—as plainly as she could. You're next!"

"There is no time for discussion," Cassius said. "If Miss Bondy is not there within five minutes, Ray Baxton will be killed and his body will never be found. I assure you, Miss Bondy, Karlov is desperate. He is in a state of terror over these killings. He wants to leave this island, but he will call it quits only on that condition—that you assure him that he will not be prosecuted or harmed in any way. He is to be permitted to go with you on your schooner, with the rest of these people, as far as the northern tip of Celebes. That is the other condition."

"I'll go," Marthana gasped. "I'll talk to him."

Sam started to argue, but she would not listen to his arguments. She had, she declared, gone this far, and she was prepared to go farther. She believed that Cassius was telling the truth. They had come here to save Ray Baxton's life, if possible. This was the last chance. Luck had actually played into their hands at last!

She went to the door and said quietly, "Come on, Cassius."

"No," he said. "I am to stay here. I am to see that these men do not go with you. Karlov is afraid they will try to double cross him. You are to go alone. You are to knock five times slowly on the bars.

"He will answer with five slow knocks from inside, and you will answer those with three quick knocks. You will talk to him through the bars. You will not have to go inside. Talk to him, give him your assurance, and that is all."

"Okay," Marthana said crisply. "Are those terms okay with you, Sam? To put Karlov and his gang ashore on Celebes in return for Ray Baxton's delivery to us alive?"

He said suspiciously: "Will Karlov turn Baxton loose at once?"

Cassius croaked: "She will return here with Ray Baxton. That is the entire agreement."

When Sam still refused to give his sanction, Marthana said hysterically: "Okay, Cassius! Okay, and thank God!"

And she walked rapidly away. Cassius waited. He waited perhaps ten seconds—until her footfalls could no longer be heard. Then he snatched the automatic out of his holster and said, in that croaking voice:

"One cry out of either of you and I'll kill you! Put your hands up! Both of you!"

Both Sam and Rufe started to reach for their automatics, but it was too evident that this living skeleton meant what he said. That unholy glow in his eyes now meant something. It meant that this was a trap.

It meant that Marthana, on her way to keep that rendezvous with Karlov—

Something suddenly went clicking home in Sam's brain. *A cat's claw is as swift as the swiftest steed!* The message that Koori had died to deliver had suddenly a sharp and utterly dismaying meaning. The mystery of Murder Island was magically and shockingly cleared up, entirely explained!

And Marthana was on her way out to meet death! Fearlessly, she was walking into the very hands of death!

31

THE END OF KARLOV

CASSIUS SAID: "TURNAROUND! Kneel down! Face that wall!"

"What for?" Sam said sullenly.

"No questions! Obey me or I'll shoot you down!"

Sam said, this time in a voice simulating anger: "Don't argue with him, Rufe! He means what he says! He'll shoot you like a dog! Get down!"

"Skipper, I ain't arguing with no bullet."

Sam did not know whether this mild little trick was working or not—to make Cassius believe that Rufe Pound might do something obstreperous and unexpected. He counted on it to distract the living skeleton's attention for a split second.

He made the split second pay fabulous dividends. He saw the sunken eyes swing sharply to Rufe, the automatic swing a little in accord. Then Sam dropped, spun half about and dived in one continuous flow of lightning-like action.

The automatic did not go off. His flying tackle caught Cassius just above the knees, sent him flying into a table which upended as swiftly as if it were pivoted, and as he came up he drove his fists into the living skeleton's gaunt belly.

The automatic dropped to the floor where Rufe, diving as Sam had done, covered it with both hands.

Sam scrambled to his feet, saw that Cassius was almost unconscious from those blows in the belly and barked: "Watch him, Rufe!"

Sam sprinted out of the door. There was enough light now for him to see his way. He ran at top speed, pulling out his automatic as he ran. Through the trees, he saw Marthana at the door of blackbeard's castle. She was standing there in an attitude of listening, with one hand upraised.

Karlov had evidently not opened the door to her knock. And as Sam sped toward her, he saw why, quite as he had expected.

The tall, bat-like figure was just behind her, creeping toward her with outstretched arms, its black hood up about its face, its black robes soundlessly moving as it advanced on this, its final kill.

Sam stopped just long enough to aim and fire once. The sound of the explosion, shattering the silence of the dawn, made Marthana spring back from the door and spin about.

She saw the bat-like thing coming toward her, and she screamed.

Sam shouted: "Karlov! Stand where you are or I'll kill you!"

The man in the black cape and gown turned. Sam caught a glimpse of the insane blue eyes, dazzling even in this half-light. The man whirled and ran toward the hill.

Sam hesitated and fired again. Something was detached from the running figure—and it looked like a long black rod.

As Sam ran past Marthana, she cried: "Sam! Stay with me!"

But he ran on. He only glanced at the black thing on the ground as he followed Karlov up the hill. It was what he had expected—a pair of remarkable tongs with tremendous leverage. With these, in their prickly black covering, Karlov had crushed the necks of his victims. It was these tongs that Sam, with their five fingers, four on one side, one on the other—had felt at his own neck that night.

A little farther up the hill he passed the footgear Karlov had worn—long wooden sandals with leather straps. With these Karlov had made those baffling marks in the sand. The stench of corrupt flesh, Sam suspected, had not had to be imitated. Any chunk of rotting meat would have sufficed. He detected nothing of the kind now.

THE KILLER HAD disappeared over the top of the hill. When Sam reached the crest, Karlov was running toward the spring. Sam shot again as the man in the black hood rushed past the spring and continued along the crest of the hill.

That shot must have reached its mark, for suddenly Karlov uttered a scream of terror or rage. It was a hideous sound. It was a blood-chilling cry, but it did not cause the red-headed man to hesitate.

He shouted; "Karlov! Stop or I'll kill you!"

But the fleeing man did not even pause. As if in answer, he screamed again, and this scream was suddenly echoed by shouts from below.

The objective of the fleeing man was puzzling to Sam, but not for long. The hill ended sharply in a cliff, with a drop, almost sheer, to the ground of about eighty feet.

Sam did not fire again. As he ran in pursuit, he saw the bat-like figure fly into the air, just as it had seemed to do last night when he chased it and lost it. Then, screaming once again, the figure in black dropped from sight.

When Sam reached the brink of the cliff, Karlov was lying at the foot of it among the rocks that were strewn there. He was lying on his back, certainly dead, with his eyes staring straight up, his mouth open. His body was twisted so that it was apparent to Sam that his back was broken.

Sam stared down at him a moment, breathing rapidly, then turned about and retraced his steps to the spring, and on down the path to blackbeard's castle. Marthana was still standing at the door, but the others who had been drawn by the sounds of shooting were walking away, toward the base of the cliff—Hiram Fillow, the twins and the bobbed-haired woman. They were walking rapidly.

The blond girl, with her back to the bars, was fighting not to faint. She gasped: "Where is he?"

"At the foot of the cliff."

"Dead?"

"Yes. He jumped."

"It was Karlov, Sam! It was Karlov!"

"Yes," he said.

"He was going to kill me!"

"With this. This is the cat's claw."

He showed her the tongs, and she shuddered. She chattered: "We've got to get Ray!"

"I'll get the keys."

"Oh, don't leave me alone," she said.

"You're safe now, baby. Hang on."

He ran to the house. Cassius was sitting in a chair, looking less like a living skeleton now than a dead one, and
Rufe Pound was standing over him, pale and grim and
ugly-looking with an automatic in his hand.

"The keys," Sam said.

Cassius did not question him. He handed over the keys.

Rufe puffed: "How's Marthana?"

"Okay."

"Karlov?"

"Dead. I'll tell you about it later. Tie this guy up hand
and foot. Then go out and round up the others and bring
'em here. There won't be any fight in them. If there is,
shoot."

SAM RETURNED TO blackbeard's castle. Marthana was
standing where he had left her, a pale, frightened girl, still
trembling. As Sam unlocked the doors, she said, with a
little smile: "What Jeff told me about you was too mild.
He said you were a fighter, but he didn't go into enough
details. You're good."

"Sure," Sam said. "I'm good." He threw open the doors.
"Get in there. There's nothing to be afraid of any more.
Straight ahead to those stairs."

"Okay, Skipper." He knew she was on the verge of
hysterics. She was a brave girl, but she had gone through
too much. She said shakily: "We've won, Sam. We've done
what we set out to do. But, oh, Sam, I can't help hoping
for Porter's sake that Ray's dead. He's got to be dead, Sam!
Porter's the one who ought to have the whole thing. Sam,
Sam, Ray's got to be dead!"

"Cut it out," Sam growled.

"I know it sounds terrible, but it's true. You know it's true, skipper!"

"Get up those stairs."

Marthana went up the stairs slowly, drearily, as if she had neither the strength nor the heart to climb them.

"It's just got to be, skipper. I think—I think if Ray's alive—that worthless, contemptible beast—I think I just won't be able to stand it!"

He saw that, hysterical as she was, she meant it. And he didn't blame her. She was right.

They had reached the top of the stairs. Sam took her firmly by the elbow and hustled her down the hall. At the last door on the right, he stopped. He tried a key and it worked.

"Go on in," he said.

Marthana started in with Sam behind her, watching her warily, to catch her if she fell.

A man was lying on a bed against the wall. His hands and feet were tied, and there was a gag in his mouth. But he did not have yellow hair. He had dark eyes and black hair. The gagged and bound man on the bed was not Ray Baxton.

In a thin, incredulous voice, Marthana cried: "Jeff! Oh, Jeff!"

She did not faint. She ran across to the bed and she pulled Jeff Carmichael up and folded him in her arms and began to cry.

It would take Marthana some time to recover from the shock of this. Sam had dared not tell her. He was afraid Jeff would not be alive.

She kissed Jeff before she took the gag out of his mouth.

She kissed him and hugged him and laughed and sobbed. She was suddenly radiant and strong. The transformation from that pale, shattered girl to this restored and happy young woman was amazing, and, to Sam, very satisfying.

And suddenly she said: "But where's—Ray Baxton?"

And Sam answered: "The gentleman lying dead at the bottom of the cliff is Ray Baxton."

"Not Karlov!"

"Yes."

32

JEFF'S STORY

JEFF CARMICHAEL COULD not talk at once. He could not speak at all. His mouth muscles were paralyzed from the gag, which had been in place day and night, except when he was fed, ever since the *Blue Goose* had been sighted entering the lagoon.

He was very anxious to talk, as he had a great deal to say, but most of what he had to say at first was for Marthana's exclusive benefit. He said most of it with his strong arms.

Sam sat and watched them and grinned foolishly. It was great stuff, all right. It was, without any question at all, the greatest day in his life. It was a great satisfaction to have brought about this reunion of the two people he liked better than any one in the world.

It took Marthana a long time to grow used to the fact that Jeff, so bitterly mourned for dead, was alive and well and unharmed.

Then she wanted answers to a thousand questions.

She said to Sam: "You knew Jeff was up here all the time!"

"Not all the time. Only the last few minutes. Since I figured out that message of Koori's. I finally figured out, while Cassius had us covered with his gun, that 'the steed' meant the Baxton automobile. The rest was easy. I figured Baxton had let his beard grow and dyed it and his hair black. Why he wanted all these people dead is something I can't explain."

Marthana, sitting on the bed with her arm through Jeff's, said: "It's up to you, darling."

Jeff Carmichael grinned—his famous old grin—and said in a husky, throaty whisper: "Well, I'll do my best, but it's a lot of story."

"Begin in the wireless room," Marthana said. "What happened in the wireless room that night? We thought you'd been stabbed and thrown overboard. We were absolutely convinced of it. We found blood on the deck and a trickle of it going to the rail."

"First of all," Jeff said, "I overheard a conversation between Ray Baxton and Bruno Reddy, an oiler. It didn't make much sense, but I knew something was going on. They mentioned an island, and I got the idea that Ray was plotting to kill somebody. I tried to tell you, Marthana, and then when Baxton came up I scrammed and sent the message to Sam. Then Ray came to the wireless room, pretty tight, but not as tight as he was acting, and told me I was to come along with him.

"He said we were going in the launch, and I said we were like hell. A squall was blowing up. You remember that squall. And I said no. And he said, yes, that I was in his employ, on his payroll, and taking orders from him. I said nuts to you, dearie, I am in the employ of the Radio Corporation of America. And we had a scuffle.

"I'm tough, but he was tougher. He knocked me out. The next thing I knew we were in the launch, in the squall, and

I was tied hand and foot, with a cut on my arm. There were five inches of water in the boat, and he didn't even bother to bail. He drove through the gale like the crazy man he is—was, if it's true he's dead."

"He's dead, all right," Sam said.

"That's fine," said Jeff. "If he wasn't, I'd kill him with my bare hands. Well, we rode through that squall. Next morning, we pulled in at a deserted island. It looked deserted. I don't know where it was, and I don't think I'd recognize it again. But it was evidently a place Baxton knew all about.

"He went ashore there and he came back with gasoline and food. It must have been cached there for him by this gang.

"We went on, and we stopped at other islands, generally about once a day. Baxton was a good navigator. He had a sextant along. He shot the sun and he plotted his course and he never missed a reckoning once. Why not? He's a yachtsman. It took us five or six days to get here. I lost count."

"These people," Marthana interrupted, "were expecting you, of course."

"Oh, yes. Everything was ready, and they had about a month to get their act all ready."

"Hold it a moment," Sam broke in. "Why did he want you along? Has he a wireless plant?"

"No. It's funnier than that. Do I have to tell you that he was as crazy as a coot?"

"No," Marthana muttered. "I should say not."

"He got these nutty ideas about people. He thought that all people fell into two classifications, as far as he was concerned—and he called them the blues and the reds. He

said everybody has a sort of halo, and it's either red or blue;
the blues were his friends, and the reds were his enemies.

"You had a red halo for him, Sam, but mine was very,
very blue. Do you get it? I had the bluest halo he ever saw.
That made me lucky for him. I was his lucky piece, or his
talisman. Anyhow, he figured I brought him luck. That's
how nutty he was. So when he skipped the ship that night,
he took me along—just to have my halo around, I guess.

"He kept me tied up in this room, and he used to drop
in and talk things over. I knew his whole scheme. I know
every detail of it. Can you imagine what I went through up
here, gagged and bound, while it was going on—knowing
that you were on that list, Marthana?"

Marthana snuggled against him and grinned raptur-
ously.

"Why," Sam asked, "did he want to kill her, and Rosen
and Hobb?"

"Because," Jeff Carmichael answered in that husky whisper, "they were the only people in the world who knew he
was crazy. His father's will stipulated that if Ray was insane,
the property should all go to Porter."

"Ah!" said Marthana. "*I* didn't know. That's what Rosen
and Hobb were holding out on us, Sam!"

JEFF SAID, "WELL, he thought you knew, that's why you
were on that list. Ray acted a little queer once or twice in
front of the old man, and that's why that insanity clause
was in the will. But Ray controlled himself all right until
one night shortly before we reached Bali. You see, the three
of them, Rosen, Hobb and Ray, were in the smoke room
when Ray cut loose.

"He said they were plotting to kill him. He said they

were turning into animals. The doctor was a lizard and Ben Rosen was a toad. It must have been pretty terrible. For at least ten minutes he was utterly insane, then he snapped out of it. His father was dying. It was too late to do anything, but Hobb and Rosen had ample proof—and intended to testify to it in court when they got back to the States—that Ray Baxton was insane."

"That explains Rosen, then," Sam said. "He was holding out about Ray's insanity. The rest of his story was true, except that I don't think he saw Ray get away in the launch. I think he passed out, and didn't know that Ray was gone until morning."

Marthana said slowly, "It's all so fantastic. I just can't believe that Karlov was Baxton. He fooled us all! Why, he didn't look any more like Ray—"

"It was pretty smart," Jeff said, "He was a smart guy. The beard changed the shape of his face. The black hair, curled, changed his entire complexion. He kept large pellets of cotton in his nostrils, which distended his nose and made it bulbous, and besides, it changed the tone of his voice—made it nasal.

"You see, Ray planned to kill the three of you. He wasn't going to kill Sam. He was going to let Sam find him in this room after you'd been killed, Marthana. He would wash that black coloring and the wave out of his hair, shave off his beard, and be found by Sam, tied up and gagged just as you found me. Because that beard had to come off, he never dared go out in the sun. He couldn't risk sunburn. Karlov would have permanently vanished, leaving nothing behind but mystery. You would have taken him back to civilization, and no one would be alive to prove that he was insane. His testimony about the madman, Karlov, who had kidnaped him, would have cleared these other artists. That was his entire plan."

"Did he mention Koori?"

"Yes, often, She came here the night you landed. She was trying to blackmail him for a million dollars. It was her father's scheme. She was merely carrying out orders. It seems that this whole scheme was hatched during the confusion of Oliver Baxton's death and burial in Bali. There was a yearly temple dance going on—a famous festival.

"This girl Koori lived on a near-by island and came with her father to see the temple dance. So did this gang here— the twins, the blue-haired gal, Miss Mendoza and the old fellow with the funny teeth. They were an artistic, radical bunch that had come to Bali to escape the horrors of modern civilization, but they went broke on Bali.

"They came to Ray Baxton and begged him to found a colony for them, and finance it. Ray hatched this scheme— the whole scheme—and put it up to them. Each of them was to get a cold half-million if the scheme succeeded. Koori and her father overheard the discussion, got all the details. And Koori was sent along on this cruise to contact Baxton and blackmail him. That's why he killed her. But not entirely why.

"She had fallen in love with you, Sam, and Baxton was afraid she'd spill the beans. That's why he killed Faustine Fife, too. She'd fallen for that handsome doctor, and Baxton was afraid she'd break down and blab when he killed the doctor."

"How about this man, Mace Littlejohn, who was buried

the day we got here—the first one Baxton killed with those horrible tongs?" Marthana asked.

"Mace Littlejohn gave him his inspiration," Jeff answered. "Mace Littlejohn died during a heart attack that was brought on by a discussion of Baxton's scheme the night before you arrived. It gave Baxton his idea. The tongs were here, with a lot of junk left behind by the British pearling company that used this island forty or fifty years ago.

"He crushed Littlejohn's neck with them, to try them out. His idea was to scare the daylights out of the lot of you the minute you landed—to get you into a state of wild-eyed confusion—and then to kill you off, one by one, as fast as he got the chance. Did they tell you that Karlov's daughter and Mendoza's brother had been killed by the beast?"

"Yes," Sam said.

"That was part of the build-up. There were no such people. Ray Baxton was insane, but he was the smartest crazy man that ever lived."

"How about that oiler—Bruno Reddy?" Sam asked.

"That rat! He was on the payroll, too. The night we left the yacht, Baxton's orders to Reddy were to cripple the engine enough so that the yacht couldn't hunt for the launch, and when the Victory searched Singapore, to cripple the engines properly, so that she'd be laid up for weeks or months. He didn't want that yacht coming here. Too much of a crew. He figured Rosen would have to charter a schooner like Sam's. In fact, he may have had Sam's schooner in mind. He knew I'd sent Sam that telegram to meet me in Singapore. He may even have figured that Sam would definitely bring you here in the *Blue Goose*. I'd told him about you, Sam. He knew all about you. What happened to that oiler?"

Sam briefly described the oiler's death in the harbor.

"Did a fellow named Chester Cave," Jeff asked Marthana, "contact you in Singapore?"

"Yes. He wanted fifty thousand dollars for a chart showing where this island is."

"That checks. He went off in the boat they came here in. That fifty thousand he'd collect from you was to be his cut."

"He didn't collect," Sam said. "We got the chart away from him. Then he tried to contact me later and Reddy killed him. I think he had decided to tell me everything— for a price—and Reddy was on his trail to see that he didn't."

Jeff said: "Are there any more questions? If so, they can wait. I want to breathe some fresh air and see something but the walls of this room!"

"One more question, darling," Marthana said. "What was to become of you?"

"That's easy," Jeff said lightly. "My halo was almost worn out. I was going to be killed and buried early this morning!"

33

JUSTICE

RUFE POUND HAD captured the stunned and bewildered members of the art colony at the base of the cliff where Ray Baxton's body lay. He had herded them, at the point of his automatic, back to the house, and was holding them there when Sam, Marthana and Jeff arrived. They were no longer quite so stunned or bewildered, and the bobbed-haired woman said, when Sam came in:

"We're not standing for any rough stuff, redhead."

Rufe Pound blurted: "Who's the guy? That ain't Ray Baxton!"

"My old pal Jeff Carmichael," Sam said. "You're going to strain your brain over this. Take it easy and we'll tell you all about it when we get on board."

The old turkey gobbler burst out: "What do you think you're holding us for?"

Sam gazed, one at a time, at the four belligerent faces.

"Watch them, Rufe," he said, and then answered the question: "I'm going to hold you as accessories to the crime of the century. This is Dutch territory, and the nearest territorial court is Batavia, Java. I'm going to turn the five of you over to the Dutch authorities there."

Anita Mendoza blazed: "Like hell you are!"

"Watch them, Rufe. Marthana, she packs her gun in the top of her left stocking. Get it."

The bobbed-haired woman started to reach for it, but changed her mind. She submitted to the indignity of Marthana's relieving her of it. But she said: "You're wasting your time taking us to Batavia, or anywhere else. We had nothing to do with this mess. We came here to set up a colony—"

"Nuts. You came here to help Ray Baxton for a half-million bucks apiece. You knew these killings were going to take place. One word from any of you would have stopped them. You're responsible for the deaths of Ben Rosen, Dr. Hobb, Miss Fife and Koori. You let both those girls be killed. You could have stopped it. You're a pack of yellow-livered rats. Hanging's too good for the lot of you."

The bobbed-haired woman bleated: "You wouldn't let a woman hang!"

"The hell I wouldn't! I'm going to stay in Batavia and I'm going to sit there and smoke a pipe when they spring the trap under you. Koori was worth a thousand of you. You let that maniac kill her. You let him murder your pal—the only decent one in the lot of you! What makes you think I'm going to show you any mercy?"

Anita Mendoza shrieked: "You can't prove it! You can't prove a thing!"

"Sister, this gentleman here—" He indicated Jeff, tall and grim beside Sam, with a look in his eyes as ruthless, as hard as that in Sam's green eyes. "And this lady here—" He indicated Marthana. "The three of us are going to testify the five of you to the gallows. We knew your story from start to finish. Turn around, all of you. Face that wall. Anybody who doesn't want to wait for the hangman can make a quick move now. Rufe, tie 'em up."

Sam examined Cassius's bonds to make sure they were secure. When the captives were bound, Sam and Jeff went to the foot of the cliff.

Marthana had no stomach for the further presence of Karlov, even in death. And she had no curiosity.

THEY FOUND THAT Karlov's—or Baxton's—neck and back had been broken by that fall. He had died instantly. They undressed him, and they found that all three of Sam's shots had been hits. One bullet had lodged high in the left thigh, another in the upper part of the left arm, the third in the right shoulder. Any one bullet should have stopped him.

Jeff said: "Do we bury him or leave him for the buzzards?"

"Neither. We pickle him and take him back to civilization. This stiff is worth exactly eight hundred million dollars, just as he is, to Porter Baxton. One reason we came here was to get proof that this guy was dead or alive—proof that would stand up in court."

"Photographs?"

"No. As Ben Rosen said, we need the corpus delicti. You are now looking at the most valuable corpse that ever died. Take a good look, boy. You will never again see dead meat worth around four or five millions dollars a pound!"

The unpleasant task of pickling the corpse of Ray Baxton fell to Rufe Pound, because the mate inadvertently admitted that he had once worked in a fishery where fish were pickled, or put down in brine.

One of the three casks which Sam had bought in Singapore for the purpose of smuggling his three passengers aboard the *Blue Goose* that eventful night was used for the purpose.

Ray Baxton, in brine, was taken to Batavia. There the body, in its cask of brine, was surrendered to an amazed and somewhat horrified American consul. And in Batavia Sam turned his five prisoners over to the Dutch authorities. Not a vengeful man, except when his deepest sentiments were affected, he remained heartless to the end. The death of Koori had moved him more deeply than anything that had ever happened to the red-headed man. She had sacrificed her life to warn him.

He had no pity for Ray Baxton's co-conspirators.

He would have prosecuted the long and dreary case against them personally, but he did not speak Dutch fluently enough. Jeff Carmichael was the star witness in the case of the Dutch Colonial Government *versus* the five artists. And he was as ruthless as Sam.

The five were not hanged. In the United States, or in a United States colony, they would have been hanged. The Dutch are a little more lenient in such matters. All five, however, received life sentences.

Jeff and Marthana departed at once to America for their honeymoon, and Sam Shay picked up his life where he had dropped it when that radiogram from Jeff reached him in Penang.

The case of Ray Baxton was finished forever, he thought, until a letter, sent by airmail across the Pacific, caught up with him in Rangoon. It was written on the letterhead of the Baxton Corporation, Detroit, Michigan. It read:

My Dear Captain Shay:

I wish to extend to you my sincere thanks for your heroic efforts which resulted in the clearing up of the mystery surrounding the disappearance of my unfortunate brother, Ray Baxton.

As a slight token of my appreciation, I have instructed my cashier to draw to your order our check in the amount of fifty thousand dollars ($50,000), which you will find enclosed herewith.

With renewed assurances of my esteem, I remain,

Cordially yours,

Porter Baxton, President,

Baxton Corporation.